SQUID SOUP

Cover and illustrations by Peter Balestrieri
Afterword by Richard Meade
Design by Emory Mead

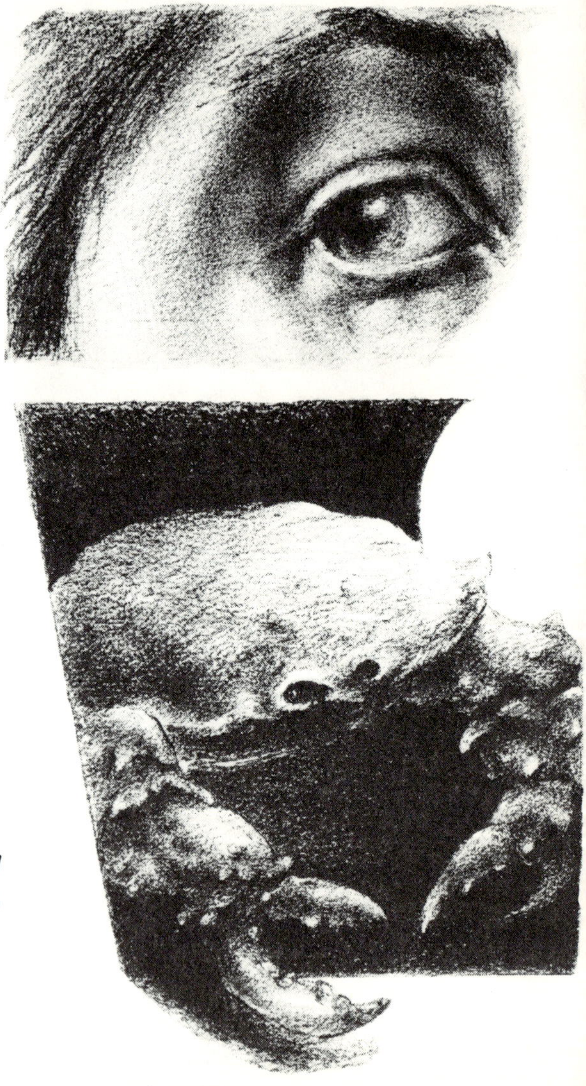

Story Press

P. O. Box 10040
Chicago, Ill. 60610

Squid Soup

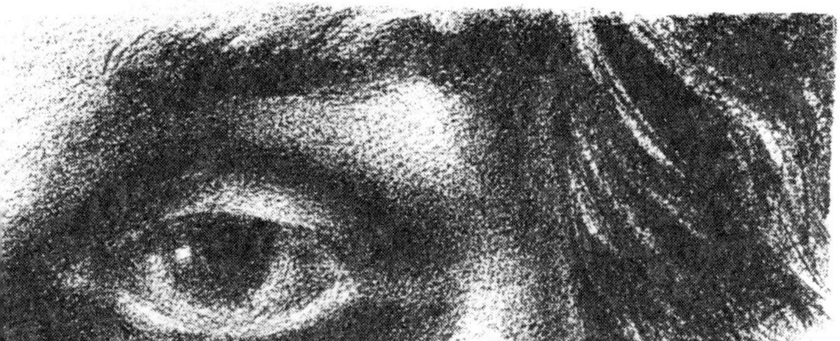

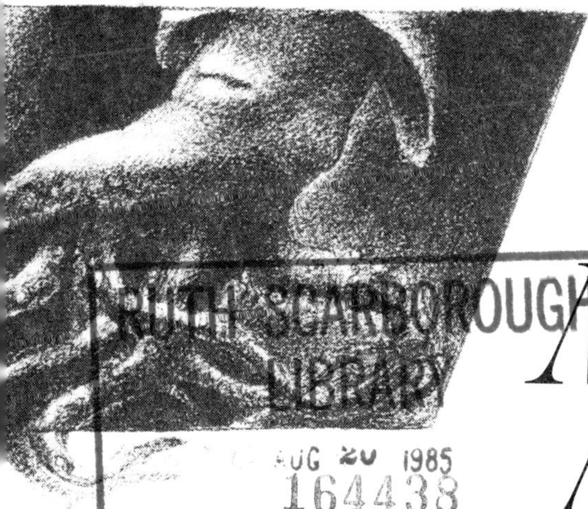

stories by Michael Mooney

Acknowledgements

Some of the stories in this book appeared originally in the following magazines: "The Strange Heart" in *The Louisville Review;* "Footings for the Humanities" in *Cream City Review;* "The Popcorn Stand" in *Colorado Quarterly*. The author is grateful to these magazines for permission to reprint.

Library of Congress Catalog Card Number: 80-13000

Printed in the United States of America
A First Edition

Library of Congress Cataloging in Publication Data

Mooney, Michael.
Squid Soup.

CONTENTS: The strange heart.—Footings for the humanities.—Chicory. [etc.]
I. Title.
PZ4.M818395Sq [PS3563.05655] 813'.5'4 80-13000
ISBN 0-931704-05-7
ISBN 0-931704-04-9 (pbk.)

to Kathy

Five windows light the caverned man.

—William Blake

CONTENTS

The Strange Heart

THE lamp cast brownish light over the bed where Leah lay. The room was dim, cavernous, and the windows along the west wall, whose shades had not been drawn, gleamed blackly. A few snowflakes tapped on the pane, and as she stared out there she saw the elm tree with its bare arms. It had come closer to the window and the house, and now it nodded, beckoning to her.

She was hot, and then she was cold. Then she was hot again. The bed was strewn with books and crayons and paper dolls. A tray of food which she had not touched sat on a table nearby. Below in the kitchen her parents were having dinner. She heard her father's low rumble, and her mother's voice was like the wind outside.

Her mother had spent the day with her reading stories, and when her father came home he had brought more stories from the library. She had chosen a tall picture book which she now held between her knees. The rest of the books had fallen off onto the floor. She stared at the black rectangle of glass.

She turned over on her side, aware of an avalanche of crayons and magazines going over onto the floor behind her, and pressed the book between her legs. She saw figures from the book on the wall. She was hot all over, and she wanted to throw off the covers, to sip the water in the glass on the tray.

The figures moved before her, men with bird faces, with leopard skins, with spears and shields. They moved between a high city with a burning tower there on the wall, and a beach which was the sill of the window. The waves were black, like the window, and sometimes one of the men died on the stones of the shore.

It was a dream, but she was not dreaming. She saw the clock, the curtain by the window, the gleaming dark glass. She stared at the picture she was seeing superimposed on the room she knew, and remembered a train ride when the inside of the car appeared on the window glass as she looked out at the passing country.

She knew she should be afraid of the dark waves, of the tower burning there in the darkness outside, but she was not afraid. In the book sometimes the men died because of the swords and spears. There were girls in the book, too, but they did not die.

Now she was cold. She would have pulled the covers around her, but the covers were around her, and her arm underneath was heavy like wood. The covers were heavy, too, like someone lying down on top of her. When she was hot the book was cool, and now when she was cold the book was hot, and she clutched it to her, hugging it with her arms and legs. It felt good.

Her father had promised to read the book after dinner. He had showed her the pictures of the men and of the tower and of the big horse and of the waves. One of the girls was big, too, and when Leah asked why, he said she was a goddess.

"What's a goddess?" she said then.

"It's like God," he said.

"What's that?" she said, and even as she asked she was too tired, and her voice faded.

She was too tired to hear an answer. She stared up at the dim and gloomy ceiling, aware of her father standing over her; aware that he was talking, although she did not hear the words.

She held the book between her legs. It was warm, and she was cold. Or was it cold and she warm? The snow came tapping at the window pane, a brittle sound like sand. The ceiling was far, very far away. It felt good. . . .

She heard snow, and then it was not snow, it was her father, and she was awake. The room was different—he had drawn the shades.

"Don't, honey," her father said. "Honey, don't."

She did not know what he was talking about until he tried to take the book away, and then she felt how tightly she pressed it to her.

"Here," he said, putting out his hand. "Don't you want me to read it to you?"

"I like it," she said.

"You're better now," he said. "I'm glad. Let me read the book."

He made to sit down on the bed beside her, pushing the cat away who had curled up against her feet. The cat slid off the bed, stretched, yawned, and sat down to look at him, blinking her eyes. Leah held the book against her and moved it up and down, looking at her father.

"Here, you've got to cover up," he said, pulling the book away. "You can't cover up like that. Now, cover up. You want to get well, don't you? Don't you want to feel good?"

"I do feel good," she said.

"Have you been reading?"

"No."

He looked at her. She looked at the drawn shades.

"I want the dark," she said.

"Do you want to sleep?"

"I want the dark. You stay."

"How can I read in the dark?"

"Tell it. From your mouth."

He switched off the light and sat down on the bed beside her.

"Give me the book," she said.

"How can you see the pictures with the light off?"

"Tell."

She was impatient, a little imperious. She felt the cat jump back on the bed and press the covers down before she lay there beside her feet. She heard the cat lick herself.

"It started a long time ago," her father said, "in a country called Greece."

"I know that," she said. "Give me the book."

"I can't find it in the dark."

"Turn on the light," she said. "I like it. It makes me feel good."

"Rest makes you feel good. And water. Drink some more water."

He reached for the water glass, but she pushed his hand away so that he spilled.

"I won't, unless you give me the book," she said.

"You want the light out, and you want to read the book—you're a strange little girl."

"I don't want to read. I'll show you—"

"Are you a cat like Moon?" he interrupted. "Can you see in the dark?"

She made to reach for it, but he stopped her hand.

"I know what's best for you," he said. "Now, cooperate a little bit. Don't get yourself excited."

"Tell."

"Don't get yourself upset."

"Tell!"

He cleared his throat and relaxed his hold on her hand.

"Now, where were we?" he said. "In a far-away country called Greece there lived a young girl named Leda."

"That's my name," she said.

"Leda," he said. "With a 'd'."

"I like her," she said.

"Now this Leda was very beautiful, the most beautiful girl in the whole world, and one day Zeus who was the king of the gods looked down from the top of heaven and saw this beautiful girl and loved her very much."

"Am I beautiful, Dad?"

"Very beautiful, honey."

"As beautiful as she?"

He thought a moment.

"When you're well," he said. "When you're well, you're

the most beautiful girl in all the world."

"You said she was."

"That was before. She was the most beautiful when she lived. A long time ago."

"Am I the most beautiful now?"

"That's right."

"I don't believe you."

"Well, that's all right," he said.

"You just say that to make me feel good."

"You can think that if you want," he said.

"You always say that kind of stuff."

"Well, it's true. Does it make you angry?"

"Is she dead?"

"Yes. Now."

"When did she die?"

"Long ago," he said.

"How did she?"

"I don't know."

"Does it tell in the book?"

"I don't think so," he said.

"Go on, go on. Tell."

"Well, Zeus loved this little girl very much, and he wanted to visit her, but he knew that if he went to her as he really was, and if she saw him as he really was, she would be afraid."

"Why?"

"Because he was a god, dear."

"Are people afraid of gods?"

"Very."

"Why?"

"Because they're so powerful."

"Do they hurt people?"

"Sometimes," he said.

"Why?"

"Because they're so strong."

"Did he go dressed up? In disguise?"

"As a beautiful swan."

"Go on, go on. Tell."

Her father went on talking. As she listened she reached out

to the bedside table and found a book, one that her mother read, and put it down between her legs. It was smaller, but it was heavier, and thicker, and now she pressed it there, moving it up and down. She realized that her father had stopped.

"Leah, honey," he said.

"Did she die because of God."

"Yes. I think so."

"Because He was mean to her?"

"Because He was so strong."

"Was she afraid?"

"I don't know. Maybe," he said.

"I'm not afraid—"

"Leah, honey, stop."

"Where's Mommy?" she said.

"Downstairs, with your grandmother."

"Tell her to come."

He was off the bed so suddenly that Moon let out a yell and disappeared underneath.

"I want to show her," Leah called out after.

But when her father had disappeared downstairs, it was her grandmother who first peeked her head in the door.

"Are you asleep?" she whispered.

"Turn on the light," Leah said.

"Are you better now, darling?" her grandmother said, approaching the bed. "How do you feel?"

"Good."

Her grandmother sat down beside her in the dark and stroked her forehead, pushing her hair back against the pillow.

"You feel cool now, darling. Did you drink your juice and get a good rest, to make the fever pass?"

"Turn on the light. I want to show."

Her grandmother switched on the lamp and smiled down at her, expecting a game.

"What do you want to show me, you monkey? You are better, aren't you?" she said. "Are you going to play a trick on your old Nana?"

"No," said Leah, kicking back the covers. "This."

Her grandmother looked. Her face was white.

"Stop that," she said.

"It feels good," said Leah.

"You'll irritate yourself," said her grandmother, raising her hand as if she would pluck the book away. "You'll ruin your mother's book. That's not what books are for."

Leah stopped and let the book be taken out of her hands. Her grandmother picked up the book as though to dust it off, and stood up from the bed.

"You'll injure yourself," she said. "You want to get well, don't you? You don't want to be sick, do you? You'll give yourself a fever," she said at last, hitting upon the reason.

"I am well," said Leah. "It makes me well. I like it."

Her grandmother looked at her.

"I think your mother should have a talk with you—"

"What's this that we should have a talk about?" Leah's mother said, coming into the room and looking from one to the other.

Leah was silent. Her grandmother colored slightly, didn't know what to say.

"How's my big girl?" said Leah's mother, going to the bed and hugging her. "You look awfully sad. Has your dad been telling you stories to make you all better? Has your grandma been visiting you to cheer you up? Why is my girl's face so sad?"

She made a long face herself, and at once the child brightened up and hugged her mother, said that she was better.

"The book made me better," she said, sure that with her mother it would be all right. "I told Daddy, but he wouldn't listen. I told Nana, and she said that wasn't what books were for. The book made me well again."

The two women looked at each other. Leah's grandmother raised her eyebrows.

"You'd better have a talk with her, dear," she said.

"What's this about a book?" said Leah's mother. "Which book? Show me."

"That, my dear, was the wrong thing to say."

Leah's mother looked at her and then at the child, who

waited, to know what to do.

"It's all right," Leah's mother said to Leah. "What book?"

"Leah looked at her grandmother. If it might ruin her mother's book, then perhaps she should use the book her father had brought from the library, the one about the war.

"There," she said, pointing.

"Show me," said her mother, handing it to her.

"You'll be sorry."

Leah looked from one to the other, but as her mother seemed not to have heard her grandmother, and to focus solely upon her, she took the book between her legs and showed her.

"There, now what do you think about that?" said Leah's grandmother.

"It feels good," said Leah.

"Library books are unclean," Leah's grandmother said. "You don't know who's handled them."

"I like it, Mom. It makes me better," said the little girl.

"She's your child, of course," said her grandmother. "You can raise her just as you see fit—"

For a moment Leah's mother did not know what to do.

"It's all right, honey," she said then, and kissed her. "We'll go now. It's all right. We'll go now, Mother."

She made her way towards the door, ushering her mother before her, but stopped when her daughter called to her.

"Am I the most beautiful in all the world, Mom?" the little girl said.

"What do you think?" said her mother.

"Dad said I was."

"Then maybe you are."

"Will God come to visit me?"

"Did your father say that, too?"

"No, the book."

"I'm sure," said her grandmother, "that He at least has better things to do."

"Will he, Mom?"

"You should have better things to do, too, child," said her grandmother. "To occupy your mind."

"Maybe He will, honey," said Leah's mother. "If you're lucky. Shall I leave the light on?"

Leah shook her head. She wanted the light off. She wanted the shades up, wanted to see the gleaming glass.

Her mother turned off the light, kissed her, and closed the door. Leah heard her grandmother's voice as they moved down the hall and descended the stairs. She dreamed of the fierce warriors, half man and half bird, who appeared before her now more real than the wall and chair and window upon which they were superimposed. She had not been able to show her mother really, either. . . .

She came to herself when the cat jumped back on the bed and strode towards her across the covers, purring and making sounds in the back of her throat.

"Oh, Moon, oh, Moon," she said, reaching out but not stroking her until the cat arched up to meet her hand. Then she petted her, and the cat purred, pressed the covers down with her paws, and curled up.

Leah decided to show the cat what she had discovered with the book. In the darkness the old cat looked and purred and looked away. Then she made that sound in her throat, and got up and turned in a circle, and lay down again.

"Are you dancing, Moon? Does it make you dance?"

Outside between the shade and the casement the moon cast pale bands of light which fell across the bed.

So they talked and carried on and then Moon licked Leah's hand with her rough tongue, till the little girl dreamed again of the mighty warriors, half man and half leopard, who fought with swords and spears in the gloom of the ceiling, before the dark glass.

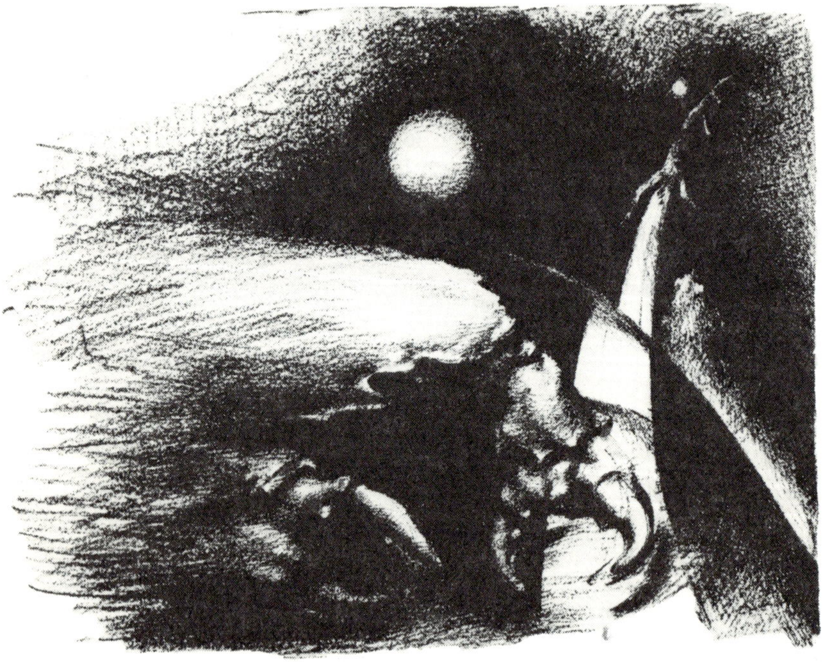

Footings for the Humanities

JOE Boulebays never intended to go to college. He intended to be a priest. He knew a guy who had gone to college, and he knew a priest, Father MacMannis, and it never occurred to him that Father MacMannis had gone to college, and so he decided to be a priest.

Father MacMannis drank whiskey in Klotski's Tavern, cursed the Green Bay Packers in front of Boulebays' Grocery, and pinched the mothers as they passed, wheeling the buggies. When Father MacMannis told Joe Boulebays that he had gone to Marquette University, Joe Boulebays decided that it had been a momentary slip, like his father's not charging Mrs. Pulaski for the milk when her husband was in the hospital drying out. He did not know how he would get to be a priest, but he decided that his best bet would be to copy Father MacMannis in every other way.

He not only drank and cursed the Packers and pinched the girls; he elaborated on the MacMannis style. He stole cars, fought in the streets, and occasionally, with his friends, gang-banged girls who were willing and able.

Any trouble in the neighborhood, and the police came to his door, which caused his father some concern. One day Representative Klotski, who was campaigning in the neighborhood, called in at Boulebays' Grocery. Klotski was very popular with the Poles and Greeks in the district because his sister ran the tavern, and he came into the store followed by a mob of reporters.

"Well, Papa Boulebays," he said, "How's the wife and kids?"

"My wife she is fine after the rheumatism which is no more, thanks to the honorable congressman and his friend the doctor. My oldest boy, Joe, I don't know. He is a constant soreness to my mind," said Papa Boulebays, shaking his head. "A constant threat and uneasiness to my heart," beating a horny fist against his chest. "I fear much for him."

"I want that boy to grow up to be a fine citizen like his father," said Klotski. "I want him to be a fine Democrat like his father," turning to the crowd and lifting his voice, "who will vote for the good man in November, the Democratic President of the United States, my friend, who will win victorious over his untrustworthy and not-to-be-spoken-of-in-the-same-breath Republican opponent. I want him to be these things, and so, Papa Boulebays, I want you to secure that he gets a fine education in order to become a good Democratic voting citizen. Send him to college."

For Papa Boulebays, who had never given the idea a single thought, the words came like a thunderbolt. Throughout the spring of his senior year, Joe Boulebays heard nothing but words about the honorable Representative who had fixed his mother's rheumatism by suggesting a trip to his friend the doctor, and who would now fix his own life and the life of the whole family with the magic of a college education.

It had never occurred to Joe Boulebays that his life needed repair. It was August before he filled in his application, complete with statement of academic intent. His notification of acceptance was accompanied by a message informing him that all dormitory space was filled, and so the day before registration he stole a car and drove to Madison to find a room. He drove idly around town for an hour or so, up State Street and down Fraternity Row, and gradually he gravitated southward, across the railroad tracks, into the area known as the Bush.

The Bush is Madison's slum, and Joe Boulebays observed the dilapidated houses and felt right at home. Then he saw a sign that advertised a room. The woman showed him the room with its iron bed, the smell of onions coming in under the door from the kitchen, and he paid her twenty-five dollars for the month and moved in.

When he described his living quarters to his parents, he added a room or two, relocated them in a middle class part of town, and remade the black woman into a nice fat Greek, and yet in his mind there was no shame in his living there. It was all pure joy.

A strange thing had happened to Joe Boulebays during his senior year in high school. Until it happened he was a typical young tough who roughed up people in alleys, read comic books, and gang-banged willing and able girls. When he fought, he was a berserker. He was no more than five foot six, but the thing that pleased him most in life was his right hook. At times he was sure that he could sock a hole in a wall. Once, on a bet, he had. But that was a motel wall. In his mind he knew he could sock a hole in a real wall. When the spirit moved him, he would. He was like Batman—when he socked, it went SOCK, in capital letters.

Once when the gang went to try out the cake-eaters on the North Shore, he had socked a hole in a guy's mouth which, it was said, took eighteen-hundred dollars to repair.

The strange thing that happened to Joe Boulebays in his senior year, the thing that changed his life, was that he discovered physics.

The physics teacher, Mr. Wokonski, had a theory about education and the student, and his theory was that you had to "grab 'em." As his homeroom teacher, he had made Joe take the course. The text was one of those large, ten-dollar jobs, big enough to cover a comic book. One fine spring day Joe Boulebays was sitting in class with his textbook propped up, reading a Superman comic, when by chance the comic book slipped down and revealed a large illustration of the concept of nuclear fission.

Joe Boulebays looked at it. There were concentric circles of varying shades, jagged like shark's teeth to suggest great violence, and the largest of these was flaming. Beneath the circles of violence was a miniature city, crushed and destroyed by the force. Within the center of the circles was the symbol $E = MC^2$.

Joe Boulebays looked at it like a pilgrim at Saint Truth. For him it was just the same as the violence in the comic, only here the magical symbol $E = MC^2$ replaced the BIFF BANG KADAZ. Even the colors were the same, white hot at the center, shading outward to red.

Nothing like this had happened to Joe Boulebays since his third grade music teacher had played the "William Tell Overture" to the class, and he had recognized the Lone Ranger. When Mr. Wokonski caught him with the comic he sent him to the dean, because if Mr. Wokonski ever tried to grab a student and then suspected that the student was not amenable to being grabbed, he grew vindictive.

When Joe Boulebays came in, Dean Yorki was busy with a student who had been caught urinating on the radiators. The dean had been trying to catch this student all winter because of the smell, and now in the springtime when the radiators were off and didn't smell anymore, he had caught him. If you urinated on the radiators in winter, they stank for three days, but in spring they smelled for only an hour or so, and the fellow had been caught because he had taken to urinating on them three or four times a day.

Then the dean had been tipped off by the cook in the lunch room who got suspicious when this fellow drank so much milk.

Joe Boulebays sat down in the dean's office, determined to figure out $E = MC^2$. He read the paragraphs concerned, but he couldn't understand the words. He swiped a dictionary from the dean's bookshelf and tried to piece the sentences together. He couldn't get a clear notion of what an atom was, but he gathered that it was small, really small. And yet from this, the book said, came all the force—from "unlocking" the atom.

He didn't understand that word "unlocking." But gradually he—a short man, a small man—realized that it all had to do with an idea that was particularly close to his heart—more with less. Much more. Much much much more with much much much less.

"Boulebays, what are you doing with my dictionary?" said Dean Yorki, crossing and recrossing his legs as if he had to go to the toilet.

"What dictionary?" said Joe Boulebays, "I'm studying my physics."

"Oh," said Dean Yorki, who was a former English teacher but who had a certain awareness of the idea of two cultures, and returned to his urinator.

"Cripes," whined the urinator, "my bladder was killing me."

"You shouldn't take in so much fluid," said Dean Yorki, who also sympathized with a weak bladder.

Joe Boulebays began reading physics at all hours of the day. At first he read with the idea that if he could master the concept of $E = MC^2$ he would become more super than Superman, and that putting his fist through a plaster wall, or some kid's mouth to the tune of eighteen-hundred bucks, would be child's play.

He didn't tell anyone what he was about, but when he saw his old chums now he would slap them on the back or punch them on the arm, imagining that even his friendly blows were growing more formidable, as indeed they were, and imagining his friends' amazement when he finally mastered the equation and revealed all by felling with a single blow the Blotnik Hotel.

Mr. Wokonski had tried to grab Joe Boulebays, had failed, had grown infuriated and vindictive, and had written him off. But when Mr. Wokonski read Joe Boulebays' final exam, he was flabbergasted. Mr. Wokonski's finals were characteristically half multiple-choice and half short-answer, and that year, because there were several particularly brilliant students in the class, who cleaned up the lab for him and worked each afternoon on a homemade, electronically-guided missile which sputtered on take-off, belched, and died, with the whole class in paroxysms of delight all over the football field, he included in the exam an optional essay.

It was for the bright ones, but when Mr. Wokonski came to Joe Boulebays' exam he found that Boulebays had opted out of the whole exam in favor of the final question. His essay was written in blunt childish scrawl, and yet, lo and behold, it made sense to Mr. Wokonski. The English was crudely simple, as if an Indian on a cowboy movie set had written it, leaving out all articles and adjectives and conjunctions, and yet it revealed a basic understanding.

This was because Joe Boulebays had very little in his head to muddle up his thinking and give him the illusion of knowing something that he did not know. In physics, Joe Boulebays was a truly educated man in the Confucian sense that his mind was empty. Mr. Wokonski found that Joe Boulebays' examination revealed not only a knowledge of the higher mathematics involved, but more important, outside reading. Mr. Wokonski reassessed his whole year with Joe Boulebays, found that after all he had grabbed him, and gave him an A; which raised two D's in English on Boulebays' record and allowed him to pass muster on the computers out in Madison. . . .

In Madison Joe Boulebays had enrolled in the usual freshman courses, but he attended only his physics lecture. There was an afternoon lab, but he never went because all theory found its application in his own mind.

He imagined his every action as involving physical laws, and then he calculated distance and advantage, weight and trajectory, in order to get the most from the least. Thus, he found with his calculations of fulcrum and distance that, if he meant to open a door, he pulled it off its hinges. If he meant to walk, he ran. In shaking hands, he crushed his friend's fingers.

It all came from physics, and yet he couldn't be sure he wasn't simply trying harder.

People grew afraid of him. He talked so loud, he laughed so hard. He had so much energy that they thought he was mad. His landlady knew that he was crazy.

Her husband was a laborer who had been laid off early that summer, and in their little house, with their seven children, they had to rent out the front room. They lived now in the kitchen and slept in the back, all together on the mattresses on the floor. The door between Joe Boulebays' room and the kitchen was akilter, and the sounds and smells passed freely back and forth. On the first night that Joe Boulebays was there, a few minutes after the children were in bed, he looked up from his physics book and realized that on the floor in the next room the man and the woman were making love.

He listened to the hard thrusting action as the man drove her across the room and up against the door. To Joe Boulebays it was wonderful. He had discovered a new realm for the use of physical theory. He gave out a cheer and beat approval on the door. Unfortunately, his cheer was a roar, and his fist went through the door.

The woman shrieked and rushed about the kitchen trying to find her clothes, while her husband stuck his big face through the hole into Joe Boulebays' room. He had an ugly look on his face, but when he saw Joe Boulebays this became a tremendous grin.

"What you doing, whiteman?" he said, grinning, pleased with himself.

"WOW," said Joe, taking a cut at the air. "POW."

They left the woman in the kitchen and went down to the corner for a beer. Few words passed between them, but occasionally the landlord, whose name was Samuel Gompers Wooten, would look at Joe Boulebays and laugh.

"Oh, whiteman," he would say. "You sompen else."

Still, Joe Boulebays knew that it had been only a door that he had put his fist through, and a no-good door at that. He tried to explain this to Samuel Gompers Wooten, using his best Indian-on-a-cowboy-movie-set-reading-a-Batman-comic-book English, and Samuel Gompers Wooten appeared to understand. Back at the house, Joe could hear him relating this in turn to his wife in what was for Joe Boulebays his best Steppin-Fetchit-reading-a-Batman-comic-book American. From that moment Mrs. Samuel Gompers Wooten knew that

Joe Boulebays was crazy. Then Samuel Gompers Wooten tried to make love to Mrs. Samuel Gompers Wooten on the floor again, with the crazy man Joe Boulebays there on the other side of the hole in the door, and she knew that Joe Boulebays had made her husband crazy, too.

But Joe Boulebays had a new object of contemplation—love. It seemed to him particularly appropriate, because in his mind it all related to that primal image of explosion, that primal concept of more with less. He had plenty of past experience which he could recount to himself, plenty of empirics to sort out and weigh, but the more he thought, the more he realized that a gang-bang was poorly related to his principle of more with less.

After all, he thought, the whole business boiled down to a kind of cyclotron. His seed was the electron, and he would bombard the nucleus. A gang-bang was a primitive form of this, very impure to his mind, and indeed his mind was penetrating into the realm of pure mechanics.

The thing about Joe Boulebays was that all the lust and thrust and explosion existed in the pure reaches of his brain. Fortunately, in that college town he was saved from the medieval malady—the blown mind which results from too much sperm having ascended into the skull—because in that town there was always a supply of young ladies who were more or less willing and able. Joe Boulebays met his particular young lady while she was carrying a sign.

There was a protest outside University Hall, and with the atoms thrusting and lunging in his brain, Joe Boulebays unwittingly crossed the picket line and received a terrific blow about the ears. For a moment he thought that it had happened—the explosion in his brain. He had at last achieved the epitome of an atomic outburst in his own body. Before him he saw this young woman waving her sign. Still, he liked to look at things in a positive light, and a minor explosion was on the right track, and he nearly belted her out of sheer joy. For the thought he received a kick in the shins.

"WOW," he cried, laughing that two minds could so operate on the same interval.

The next day as Joe Boulebays crossed the railroad tracks to his room, he saw this girl sitting on a flat car watching him. The equations in his mind, the diagrams and theories, coalesced into one empirical exercise, and he shouted for joy. She sat on the flat car, her legs over the side, and looked at him as he approached. She was a husky girl, about his own size, and his grin infuriated her.

"YOU ME," he said, when he stood before her. "SOCK BANG KADAZ."

He flailed the air, to demonstrate what he meant.

She jumped down off the car and, quicker than he could think, laid him a straight left aside the jaw.

How well in his mind Joe Boulebays had conceived this dance of love! In sheer delight he belted her backwards into the flat car, where she crumpled to the tracks, out cold.

The old man who ran the crossing gate had watched all this from the window of his shack, and now he bellowed in rage at this violation of femininity. Joe Boulebays heard the challenge and saw the old man gallop over the sidings to her defense. Boulebays marked his ground, measured the arc of his defense, and felled the crossing guard like a rotten tree with a scything blow to the chops.

Fortunately, it would be no eighteen-hundred-dollar job, because the old man had no teeth to begin with, and he would just have to buy a two-week supply of straws.

Joe Boulebays left him groveling, propped the girl on his arm, and made for home.

When he got her to his bed, she had come around, and she was bleeding from the mouth. Quickly and efficiently, according to lines of force, he ripped off her clothing. It must be said that this was the first time Joe Boulebays had ever conducted such calculated and pure exercises upon his theories, and when the experiments were complete, he knew that he had mastered the secret of the atom in his body, that he had mastered the concept of more with less—much more. He rose up in bed, shouted mightily, and from a kneeling position put his fist through the solid plaster wall so that he scratched his knuckles on the siding nails.

"You sompen else, whiteman," said Samuel Gompers Wooten, his big face grinning through the hole in the door.

Joe Boulebays grinned at the face, like the face in the canvas curtain at the State Fair that he had thrown pies at, and simultaneously the face became contorted and strangulated, then popped backwards out of the hole, and in its stead appeared the face of Mrs. Samuel Gompers Wooten. She rolled her eyes at the couple on the bed and shrieked, and the girl bolted out of the house.

Unhappily, Joe Boulebays flunked out of college at the end of the semester. He had a grade in physics, but he had incompletes in his other four courses which registered as zeros on the computer and demolished his grade point average. Happily at that time, the university began construction on a new Humanities building, and Samuel Gompers Wooten got a job, and got Joe Boulebays a job, pouring the concrete footings.

For Joe Boulebays it was the perfect opportunity, and employing every principle he knew, he became a relentless setter of forms and puddler of concrete.

Samuel Gompers Wooten was a finisher, and he received good wages, although by this time he did not need the money. In his slack period he had become a pimp, and he got the finishing job to disguise his real income. It was at this time that he had his front tooth capped in gold, for no other reason than to have the dentist cut out of the gold capping the shape of a heart, as the sign of his guild.

The Wootens moved out of the Bush at this time, too, and Samuel Gompers Wooten invited Joe Boulebays to move with them. For two months Mrs. Samuel Gompers Wooten would not move into the new house, because, as she put it, "De whiteman de Debil." But at last, just seconds before the bulldozers leveled the old homestead, she relented, and once again Joe Boulebays enjoyed the bacon-and-fried-bread atmosphere of the Wooten's room off the kitchen.

One day in March when Joe Boulebays was puddling concrete, he looked over the sidewalk fence around the excavation and saw his girl. He shouted at her, waving his shovel and calling out monosyllabic evocations of his love, and all the men looked up and cheered and hooted, and much to Joe Boulebays' dismay, she disappeared.

The next day he saw her lurking about the fence, and again when he roared out his joy, she vanished. The third day, after putting away his shovel, which he cherished, because to his mind the lever was a noble discovery, owing to its integral part in the fulfillment of the supreme principle of more with less, he found her waiting for him at the corner.

She stood there in the cold, bundled in a great coat, and eyed him with apprehension. He tried to express his delight, and in this he could not keep from rapping her on the arm a little.

"Cut the crap, Tarzan," she said. "I'm knocked up."

For Joe Boulebays, she was Saint Peter at the Gate, and in his ecstasy he took a round-house swing at the Humanities building which was not there.

Chicory

BY the time Renny drove up in the morning in the old Chevy that for so long had been the family car, the men had already gone. If there were beer cans on the desk or coffee cups and sandwich wrappers, she pushed them into the wastebasket, and then the telephone rang.

"There's no one here right now, I'll have him call you," she said. "No, the bookkeeper's not here, either, you'll have to leave your name. . . ."

Her father handled the books, and that was what he had her say. Sometimes he came in the middle of the day in his new Cadillac and took his messages into the other room and talked on the phone for half an hour. Sometimes her uncle or one of the men came in the pick-up and unloaded a wheelbarrow or loaded up bags of cement in the yard. If it was her uncle, he came into the office and asked for a cup of coffee, into which he stirred three or four spoonsful of sugar. As he drank he asked what she thought of this work and if it didn't make her want to go to college.

"I don't have to go to school all my life, do I?" she said.

"You go to school all your life, you be a nun! This way is not perfect, maybe, but someday you meet a man."

Her uncle always teased her like that, and her answer was always the same.

"No, I don't think so," she said.

Each day during the time she took for lunch she strolled along the fence amidst the daisies and chicory that had overgrown the place, or sat on the edge of the stack of rusty forms and stared off at the river which ran below that corner of the yard. If any of the men returned then, she watched them while they loaded or unloaded the truck, and though they glanced at her, they never spoke.

On Fridays her father came in after lunch and made out the checks, and once when he had to leave the checks with her, the men filed in at four-thirty, and she learned more about them in a few minutes than she had in all the previous weeks. The one named Willie had lost two fingers on his left hand—he said in the service, but everyone else said in a bar. John smelled sour, an odor she realized was alcohol, and he never spoke but only played the harmonica, so that if you talked to him, that was his answer. The handsome one named Phil when he smiled didn't have any teeth, which looked ridiculous. And Pete whose wavy hair and black eyes made him look like a revolutionary, had a voice too hollow and shrill, as if his beautiful handsome head had been hollowed out of wood.

It was a chance that made her look forward to Fridays and hope her father would go out of town again and leave the checks with her. Otherwise, she went for weeks scarcely talking to a soul except over the telephone, and those voices were impatient, abrupt, and angry. The men that Friday were relaxed and expansive, satisfied and tired and even a little drunk, and as they talked amongst themselves, the words, profane and excited and bored, stirred her in a way she did not understand.

The yard and the office were downtown, and all day there was the shriek of whistles, the profound stamping of heavy machines, the odor of the tanneries or of the chocolate factory or of the stockyards if the wind was from that direction, and the air was dusty and parched. All day she yearned for the cool shady streets, the sedate green lawns and hushed atmosphere of her neighborhood at home where there were no thundering trucks, or police sirens, or hoarse factory whistles. But in the evening when she reached the house, it was not what she had wanted after all, and she felt in the soft femininity of the place an idleness and ease not of the body so much as of the soul, which made her screw up her face and frown.

"I'm never getting married," she announced at the dinner table. "I'm getting an apartment downtown."

"The hell you say!" her father said.

When she tried to explain that it was not him she was against, the clarity of her feelings vanished in the panic of being misunderstood.

Still, after dinner when she went for a ride with her friends, it was always along the lonely pitted roads amidst the coal piles near the docks downtown, where deep lonely horns announced the movement of ore boats, where bells clanged and bridges rose to allow the passage of ships with little lighted castles on one end, and she waited in the throbbing car for the thing to pass, observing on board any signs of life which might tie it to her own.

"Look along the edge, he's drinking a soda!" she cried to her girl friends, as the ship passed before them, dwarfing buildings, the stateliness of its passage marred by the commotion of moored pleasure yachts in its wake to either side.

"Look, he's got a red handkerchief!"

With her friends she read the names—*Photinia, Gaspar Luiz*—or guessed the countries whose characters she did not know, and always she guessed India, Arabia, or Egypt.

Still, during the day, after the first few weeks she no longer wanted to meet her friends for lunch, as she had done every noon after school was out and graduation over and she had begun to work for her father. Her friends, too, seemed less inclined to drive downtown to pick her up in the heat of noon, found less to talk about in the face of the stacks of rusty forms and the little concrete building that served as an office and into whose darkness they felt reluctant to intrude, even though the air was cool in there, stirred by a fan, and beside which her father's gleaming Cadillac or her uncle's Lincoln looked strangely out of place. She preferred to lunch alone without leaving the premises, to stroll along the fence where the chicory and wild sunflowers grew, to gaze down the wild, wooded bank, a tangle of dead branches and discarded tires amidst which she had seen trilliums and wild orchids, or just sit beside the stacks of iron and feel the heat bake deep into her bones, and with her eyes closed breathe the city's muscular perfume. If anyone asked her about her job, she said she worked for her father.

The thing she hated was the telephone and the complaining, impatient, angry, or cynical voices on the other end, those people who would take out their frustration on her—as if it were her fault that her father hadn't bid the job or sent the check, as if because the concrete had cracked over the winter, or her uncle weren't there, she were to blame.

When her uncle came in and took the messages, she heard his deep voice through the door to the inner office.

"Yes, yes, I come tomorrow morning eight o'clock—you be there? I put a check in a mail today, as special favor to you. Don't forget, we got a problem, too."

Then her uncle came out looking a little ruffled and asked for coffee, and while she made it he smiled at her and said:

"Maybe someday you marry rich man, no have to work any more, hey? Lie in bed all day, eat bon-bon. You like that?"

"I'm never getting married," she said then. "Where's my father?"

Sometimes her uncle told her that her father was on a job at such-and-such an address, or seeing about a problem somewhere else.

"Well, why doesn't he come in here anymore?" she said, as if her uncle were to blame.

"He's got a lot of t'ings to do, you see," he would say to her then, looking grave. "When you got a big family, like you' father, that's lotsa responsibility."

But sometimes he just shrugged and drank his coffee and left, murmuring that he didn't know.

"Maybe he's at you' grandma's house," he murmured then.

He was being sarcastic, but once she called her grandma to

ask her how to cook kohlrabi, and before she hung up she asked for Guglielmo. That was the way her grandma said her father's name. The next voice she heard was her father's.

"What do you want?" he said.

She was so stunned she didn't know what to say.

"Bruce of Central Cement called," she read off a slip of paper. "About a bill."

"Tell him I'll get the check for him. Tell him I'm in the hospital or something. Tell him I'm out of town."

She wanted to yell at him, and she was afraid she would cry, and when he hung up she did cry, although she did not know why. From then on she called her father Willie, or Will, the way the men did, or when she was really mad, Guglielmo.

Sometimes for two days her father wouldn't come to the office, and when he did come it was only for a minute, not nearly enough time for the pile of messages she had handed him. Then she realized he didn't even pick up the phone, but just rummaged around his desk in the inner office, and if the phone rang he asked her who it was and then told her he wasn't there.

"But I told him you were here," she cried.

"Tell him I'm in the can. Tell him I just stepped out the back door."

The man on the phone knew she was lying.

"He's got three days to get that for me—you got that, little girl?"

"I'm not a little girl!"

Her father came out of his office and told her never to talk like that over the telephone, and when she told him what the man had said, he got in his car and drove away. Two days later a man came into the office and asked for Willie, and Willie wasn't there.

"Get him," the man said. "I don't care where he is—now!"

He had curly black hair, blue eyes, and a baby face, and he wore around his neck a gold cross and a gold horn. Renny picked up the telephone and dialed her grandma's, and miraculously her father answered.

She couldn't hear her father's voice once the man had grabbed the receiver, and she got up from behind her desk and walked out the door into sunlight. When she came to the end of the fence, the door slammed, and a car drove away, and with her hands on the wire she stood looking out over the surface of the river, which scintillated with light.

The next day she didn't go to work but stayed home in bed, and when her father called from the office to ask where she was, she told her mother to tell him she was sick.

"What's the matter, honey?" her mother said, sitting on the bed.

"I'm sick, that's all," she said, and turned to the wall. "Can't I even be sick?"

Downstairs the baby began to cry, and her mother stood up.

"Don't worry about it, honey," her mother said. "Maybe you should take a day off."

"I'm all right, I'm just sick. Can't I even be sick!"

The next day when her uncle came to the office, she asked him who that man was.

"Who?" he said. "Him? Oh, that's nobody."

"Does my father owe him money?"

Her uncle looked at her.

"You see in this business," he said, "when Friday comes you have to write checks, am I right? When the concrete comes, you have to buy—otherwise you got no concrete for the job. Then what do we do, lean on shovel all day? Better to stay home in bed. But in bed you make more baby, ha, ha. Then you have to work harder, like your father, with more mouth to feed, always open like a little bird crying, 'More, more, more!' "

He touched her sleeve, but she did not laugh.

"So we got lot of bills to pay, but sometime not so easy to get a money, you know. This one say, 'Wait till tomorrow.' That one say, 'You give me ulcer when you call, so now I go to hospital, can't pay you, pay doctor instead.' "

Each time he did a parody of the voice, but she did not laugh, because he had not answered her question.

"Got lotsa responsibility, you father has. Got lotsa mouths to feed. Got to pay you for a job, too—see what I mean?"

"My father owes that man money," she said.

"Him? No. We pay him."

"But he owed him money."

"What, is this a crime!" her uncle said. "That's what I'm trying to tell you. Is natural, am I right? What you want me to do, rob a bank!"

"Why did he have to come here like that?"

"Because he's an animal, who knows! Because he's *biscia*—you know *biscia?* You know snake? See, in this world there is gentleman, and there is snake. But sometimes what the snake has, you got to get. So we pay—not rob a bank. So we pay—so you don't worry so much. See how I mean?"

She had never put it together, her father and his children and his job. She had never thought how difficult it might be. Living where she lived, she had taken life for granted, and even the first few weeks of working here and seeing each day the difference between that neighborhood and this, had not brought it home to her that there was a connection and that it might be hard. But that world out there rested on this. That grace and ease floated like a flower on the surface of this, drew its sustenance here, and here was smelly and dirty and hard.

The truth of this burned in her heart, and she felt it ennoble her and lift her above the easy assumptions, the pettiness and ignorance that had typified her former self, the image of which she perceived in her brothers and sisters and their every preference and opinion. And she conceived in her heart a contempt for the flower which they were, and a love for the pond, of which she had become a part.

"I feel like a movie tonight," her mother said that evening over dinner.

Without answering or even looking up, her father told her little brother to finish his peas.

"Me hate peas," her brother announced, dropping his spoon on the floor. "Me want ice cream."

"Eat your peas," Renny told her little brother. "You're

lucky you've got anything, so just shut up."

Her father and mother looked at her. Her brother began to cry.

"Where the hell do you come off?" her father said, reaching over to rumple the young man's hair.

"But I thought—"

"Get him his ice cream."

She was too surprised to talk. She had longed to express her new-found belief, and she was astonished to have her father, of all people, rebuff her faltering attempt. "I'm on your side!" she wanted to say, but instead she stood up, spilling her plate.

"Has everyone around here gone crazy!" she shouted.

As she bolted up the stairs, her mother remarked that perhaps after the dishes they could walk down to the movies.

"I mean, if Renny's going to stay home tonight," she said. . . .

Downtown Renny took the calls and no longer heard, recorded the messages and no longer thought or felt. It occurred to her once that the man whose name she did not know had called again, that he called indeed frequently, the same rough tone, the same preemptory, knowing, cynical manner, and it frightened her that he could call and that she would not hear—like waking up from a dream to realize that your life was a nightmare.

She waited for something to happen, some catastrophe which she expected and even wanted, which would confirm what she knew and show the rest of them—her sisters and brothers—how wrong they were.

"Who am I talking to?" a voice said one morning over the telephone. "Is this Renny?"

A moment passed before Renny realized it was a woman.

"This is Delores, honey. Is Willie there?"

Her father was out of the office, Renny said, but he would return the call that afternoon. . . . Delores thought this very funny.

"Is that what he tells you to say, honey? Honestly, he's a scream, your father is. Say, what are you doing for lunch?"

She spoke with a familiarity that the younger girl wondered at.

"What's the matter, doesn't the tightwad give you an hour even? I'll pick you up in five minutes, honey. If he says anything, blame Delores."

Half an hour later a beat-up gold Cadillac pulled into the yard. It sounded as though it were dragging tin cans.

"Say, you're real cute, honey, but if you wear your hair like that, no one can see your face. Willie's got a daughter like you, no wonder he feels old."

The car had a comfortable smell of tobacco and old leather, and Delores herself smelled of Arpège, and from the first it was as if Renny had known her all her life. That was the funny thing, for although they had never met, Delores knew all about her and her family, and was either telling her about herself or asking her about her father.

". . . So I said to your father, I said, 'If you can't do any better than a Chevrolet, honey, you're in the wrong business.' I said, 'Give the Impala to Renny and buy yourself a car.' Did he fix the muffler for you, honey? I thought I'd die of asphyxiation. Where do you like to eat?"

Delores had two martinis before she went to the bottle of wine, one glass of which made Renny's head whirl in a most delightful way. It was just like Delores's talk which poured over her, telling her about herself things she never knew, showering on her an attention she longed for. There was a plate of clams and another of little slimy things you ate on a toothpick and that slid down your throat like cream, and a third of chicken and eggplant.

"We only want the best, Arnold," Delores called across the room. "Want another bottle of wine, honey? Oh, just keep smiling like that, and you've got it knocked, kid. Isn't she something, Arnold? This is Willie's daughter. You know Willie. . . ."

Across the room Arnold nodded, and when Renny looked at him he raised his eyebrows and smiled.

"Just catch that face. Right off a Greek pot, hey? Oh, honey, Willie doesn't know what trouble he's got in you. No wonder he acts like a hundred years old. What's he doing with himself, anyway?"

The question seemed to Renny very funny.

"Oh, you can tell me, honey. He's not doing a damn thing, is he? He's all the time at your grandma's. How many fellas you got now?"

"None."

This was funny, too, and they laughed.

"When I was your age I didn't have any, either," Delores said, "and you know what, I wasn't any the worse for it. But what do you do when you—you know—get the urge? Do you just go crazy?"

She said this with all kinds of winks and nods but ended up looking as if she were going to cry, and the make-up under her eyes was dark and wet.

"Yeah, crazy," Renny said.

"Oh, you kids," said Delores, "damn you kids. You got it all before you, and you don't know what it's for. If I was your age and knew what I know now, you know what I'd do? Do you know how old I am?"

"Twenty-eight?" Renny said, emptying her glass before she realized it.

Delores thought this very funny, and they laughed again until the tears came, and Renny was surprised to find her actually crying.

"Twenty-eight," she said, "if I was even twenty-eight I'd never let one of them bastards touch me. Aw, you're a sweet kid, honey—I'll bet you're still a virgin."

Renny just couldn't stop laughing, and Delores couldn't stop crying, and Arnold appeared beside them and put his fingertips on the table.

"Ladies?" he said.

Arnold, too, was very funny.

"We'll be good, Arnold," Delores said, and blew him a kiss, before she leaned across the table and, lighting a cigarette, said confidentially, "You know, once upon a time, kid, I loved your father, but now it's more like for old time's sake, do you know how I mean? He was so much fun when I knew him then. I mean, we used to have fun, but now. . . ." She looked off and screwed up half her face. "Now he's a pain in the ass," she said.

Renny choked on her wine she laughed so hard.

"And you know why?" Delores said. "You know why he's all the time at your grandma's and letting everything go to hell? He's scared. Hell, honey, he's looking at girls your age, and he doesn't know if he's too scared to do it anymore, or too old to try. Do you know what I'm talking about?"

Renny shook her head.

"It doesn't matter," said Delores. "Did they ever tell you how your Aunt Lucy went nuts one night and ate pills and your uncle fed her soap flakes till she threw up—they never told you that, did they? Your mother went crazy, too, once, I heard—they never tell you till it's too damn late. It doesn't make any difference," said Delores, blowing out the smoke. "I didn't come to tell you anything—"

"No, tell me."

Delores polished off her glass and looked at her.

"Did we eat?" she said suddenly. "Oh, yeah, now I remember. Was it any good? God, I'm famished. That's the trouble with me, I'm always eating. Do you know the joke about Little Red Ridinghood? I've got a dirty mind. Some people say it's my only asset. Gee, you've got a sweet figure, honey. I was going to tell you to forget about it, the whole sex thing, and find someone you can talk to, but that's no good, either. I was going to tell you to find a guy with a sense of humor, who's not afraid to talk to a woman, but your dad had a sense of humor once, and look at him now. The trouble is when you're my age, you know what a guy is just by looking at him, but you don't know how to explain it, and you don't know if it makes any difference, anyhow. You've just got to live a little, and then you find out. You've got to make a few mistakes—it's not the end of the world."

"Hi, sweetheart, how's every little thing?"

Renny looked up, and standing by the table touching Delores' arm was that man. He wore a silk shirt open at the throat to reveal the gold cross and the gold horn that hung around his neck, and he took off his sunglasses and smiled at Renny.

"Get your mind out of the gutter, Vince," said Delores. "This is Renny—Willie's daughter."

"I don't believe I've had the pleasure," Vince said, "and it certainly would be a pleasure."

"Well, maybe for you," Delores said, "but not for anybody else on the premises. Are you going to pull up a chair, or are you just going to stand there hoping we'll notice how your pants fit?"

"I seem to recollect a certain night," Vince said, "when a certain lady found a certain pleasure—"

"We've all got our shortcomings, honey," Delores said.

"And mine ain't so short," said Vince.

"And mine is brains," Delores said. "So have a glass of wine."

But Vince begged off.

"Maybe another time," he said, bowing towards Renny and backing away. He rolled his eyes in the direction of Delores. "Sometime when your old mother's in hospital, maybe, with two broken legs," he said.

"Don't worry about him, kid," Delores said. "He's scared to death of women; that's why he talks the way he does. Do you think he's cute?"

Renny watched as he passed through the tables, and he had a funny way of swinging his shoulders when he walked.

"He reads comic books," Delores said, "and thinks he's tough. He's not so bad, really."

"Is he in the Mafia?"

"That's what I mean," said Delores. "He reads comic books. . . . You really don't know the score, do you, honey? Why do you think they act the way they do? Why do you think they get that funny damn look on their funny damn pusses? The Mafia! I'm talking about men—that's the Mafia! But it's you and me they're scared of, honey. Let's get out of here, I'm late."

Renny was late, too, and she was also drunk, and her father was furious until she said she'd been with Delores. Then he shut up and went into his room, and she could only wonder at the power this woman had who had entered her life so suddenly and completely that it felt as if she had always been there.

She didn't understand the things Delores said, but she felt she had taken on something of her power, and the funny thing was that when those hot, impatient voices called on the telephone now, she would know what to say.

Just then the phone rang, and she answered it before she thought—"Hi. What can I do for you?"—and giggled at the clumsy imitation of Delores.

"Plenty," said the voice. "It's me—Vinny. Let's start with tonight."

Thief

At night after dinner in the Pentanglia household, Joey's father would tell about the good old days when he was bodyguard to Al Capone. As many times as he told the story, Joey's grandfather would pipe up from the corner where he sat that in his day he didn't need no Al Capone, that he went all over the world and on to every foreign shore where you might meet black men or red men or yellow men or blue, who believed in salt for their god, or the horn of rhino—anything to make a man a devil. And he had taken what he wanted, he said, wine and women and gold, and sometimes he had fled in the middle of the night and rowed all day on a leaden sea underneath the blazing sun, and by himself he didn't need an army.

His grandfather's words were passionate and shrill, and they were meant to show what a sorry state his seed had come to in the person of his son, who relied on gangs and reputation—mere feathers, womanish toys.

While they talked, Joey's mother cleared off the table, or served coffee, and said not a word, for it was not the place of women to talk. But always her presence brought fresh denunciations from Joey's grandfather, or from his father loud laughing contempt for the frailty of old men's flesh.

The way they carried on in that woman's presence, you would think that Joey's grandfather had once loved someone about her size and shape who had left him for the foolish promises of a younger man, or that his father feared for his own mortality, and the ease with which a man's luck can change, and fate and the world go against him—just like a woman's heart.

She was a beautiful, olive-skinned woman, Joey's mother was, who wore her soul on her face, as the saying goes, and his father would have been handsome if his eyes had not been so wide to make him look like an ox, and his grandfather was all dry wood like the ribs of a boat that had washed up on a foreign shore to whiten in the sun. Always when their voices rose, she cried out that she was going to faint, and sometimes she did faint, and they carried her to her bed.

In the bedroom where a blue altar candle burned, she lay beneath the ancient headboard, and her chest fluttered, and a little whistling came from her throat, and she took her son's hand in hers and begged him to be a good man and not a bad man when he grew up, and to pray for her soul where it was going after this life, and God knows the things she had done that needed a son's prayers, and she begged him to be a priest.

"What's a priest," his father said, "but another kind of thief who robs from the poor and says it's God's grace!"

"A church is just another gang," his grandfather told him, "and a priest is a warlock—like your father."

When his mother said she needed prayers for her soul after the things she had done in this life, his father laughed, and remembered the time the police had come to the door and she had burned the money in the basement.

"A grocery bag full of Andrew Jacksons she burned down there," he said, "while I was telling the cops I'd been laid up in bed with the gout. With that money I wouldn't live in no dump like this," he said, gesturing towards the kitchen where the Amtrak passed the door. "I wouldn't wait for my dinner in the company of an old man and a fool," he said, looking from his father to his son.

"If she hadn't burned those bills," the old man said, "you'd have done thirty years instead of ten. But a man who relies on the intelligence of women—I pity him. A woman's brain is loosely woven. The endless waves, the boiling sun, the habits of black-skinned men who dance all night upon their father's graves—for these things a woman is unprepared."

"Like an old man's private parts," the other said. "That's why he keeps them private."

Joey's grandfather gazed out the window at the alley between the houses, with the little squares of sunlight at one end.

"Better than to expose himself to infamy," he said, "with Banker Murphy's daughter."

Joey's father went red as a brick, but a sly smile stole across his mouth, and he said there was more than one way to rob a bank, and first you put your hand in the daughter's purse, and that way you grabbed the father by the jewels.

They talked this way, each one out of the fears that life had given him for the survival of his seed. For as hard as their words were, there lay behind them a glimmer of recognition that they were all in the same boat upon the waters of this world and that sometimes the way to make a fellow trim the sail or pull an oar was with kicks and blows instead of sweet words and honey.

"What do you think a banker is," Joey's father said, "but a thief with a white shirt who has from the government a paper in Latin that says, 'Horseface gets permission to steal.' "

But in his corner the old man said the word was Coward and not Thief, for Coward hid behind a gang or a license or a law, but Thief, he took what he wanted and didn't give a damn. And if he wanted a girl, then he took her, but if he wanted her father's money, he didn't bother her with a lot of hearts and flowers but went and shook the fellow by the heels until his pockets emptied out. That was what Thief did, for Thief was a man.

They spoke not to each other but to Joey, his father with a contempt for innocence that is only natural to a man his age, his grandfather with an old man's hope in one last thing upon this earth which had proven such a sorry state, and they didn't talk long before his mother from the bedroom called in a tremulous voice, as if death itself had perched on her chest, and she couldn't catch her breath.

"Joey, please, a soda in a spoon," she called. "Joey, please, a cup of water."

That was what she craved when the burning illness took her, because her husband didn't believe in doctors—"Thieves in white coats who will cut out your liver if they find an onion and want to make a sandwich."

So Joey's mother took soda in a spoon, and while she mixed and sipped as if she were too weak to do it any faster, she whispered to the room at large that someone must pray for the soul of her who in this life had lived so wickedly, and she cast her glittering eyes upon her son and begged him to be a priest.

"Priests," his grandfather said. "Thieves without character. Defilers of women's minds."

Here was one point upon which father and grandfather agreed. And there were others as well, such as to trust no one, for he who was your friend when the sun shined was your foe at night, and that was why you had to use duplicity, his father said, although his grandfather said not to mince words or bandy looks but to tell a man straight out what you thought of him, and the devil take the rest. Tricks he left to women, who lacked resolution and used treachery to cover their weakness, whereas he himself admitted no weakness, and here he thumped his heart till he coughed like a horse, and his bones rattled in his chest.

Joey's father laughed till the tears came "to hear an old fool rattle in his throat."

"What, am I simple!" he cried. "Don't I see with my eyes, smell with my nose, the way the world is? Was I born yesterday? Did I fall out of a tree?"

He touched the old man's shoulder and sent him sprawling across the room on his ear, and there came into the old man's face a look of astonishment such as Joey had never seen, to find himself so weak and insubstantial, of no more weight and heft than a doll.

If Joey loved his grandfather, he had to listen to his father, for if the one was heroic in his philosophy, so the other was impressive in his person, who could back up what he said with kicks and cuffs and blows. If his grandfather had for him hope and a kind thought, so his father proved right about a great many things. Still, he could not lie without deeming it cowardice, and yet to stand up to the world, as his grandfather would have him do, and outface with the singleness of his purpose all creation—it was a course of action suited to more heroic times, when a man could row all day and night underneath a blazing sun or a thousand frozen stars.

Joey became a thief and left praying to others. In passing by a window if he saw a candlestick that struck his fancy, or a bowl of fruit, he opened the front door and took what he wanted, and the same went for Banker Murphy's daughter who had black eyes and white arms, and even for the headboard of her father's bed where he lay her down and himself on top of her, because she was ripe to his tooth as fallen fruit and because he cared not, as other men did, for her father's gold.

That is, he did not care for gold until he spied her father's watch upon his desk, for in his mind he scorned base metal but marveled at the fineness of a made thing, a wrought and jeweled perfection worthy to adorn his person.

"You would steal my father's watch?" Rita Murphy said, when she saw him touch it.

An impulse came over him to conceal his desire and win her approval, but this he scorned as he remembered his grandfather, and he dropped the watch into his pocket. In that little act he won her heart, for never had she met so audacious a man, and when he ripped the headboard off her father's bed, it made her spine shiver, for it was token of his triumph, and she belonged to him.

It is a fine thing to belong to the bravest man alive, especially if he has curly hair and olive skin and wears his soul on his face just like his mother. Especially if he eats black olives on his bread and red wine in his soup and loves the taste of squid and conch and octopus that crawl along the sea, which betokens woman. How could a banker or a lawyer, with his reasons and his rules, compare? A man whose hands were smooth as silk, how could he compare?

She had been to the homes of young men, had eaten roast beef at their tables, and none had a mother with a soulful face who wore a plain black dress, or a grandfather who touched her flank as if she were a prize mare worthy of the purchase, and dunked his bread in wine, and jabbered in Italian. None had a father with a face like a bull's and none a sister who spun raw wool in an upper room in preparation for the convent and showed her face on Sundays behind a bank of window flowers. None had grandmothers and ancient aunts who spoke not in English except the words "good girl" and "nice and clean" and "not ner-vous," smiling without their teeth and feeling your breasts if they were firm and your hips if you wore a girdle.

When you ate at Joey's house you ate crab and octopus and stuffed artichokes, clams and spitini and eggplant caponatina, and Sinatra played till the house swayed with the sound of it, and after dinner the men discussed the taste of tomatoes grown in the dry volcanic soil north of Catania, and somehow every word was acknowledgement of the hard facts of life, like their thanks to Mt. Etna for the flavor of her cantaloupe, which gave the cruelest act its meaning and each gesture its weight and necessity, and without which life was not worth a dime.

No, that girl came to love Joey and his family, to weep for the hardness of their life, to admire the strength of their nature, and to understand that where the Pentanglia were, cruel necessity was never far behind.

"Do you love me, Joey?"

Of course he did, he told her.

"Why do you do the things you do, take the things you take?"

He explained it to her—how else would he get for her the things she needed?

"I don't need watches," she said. "I don't need headboards and silverware and carved picture frames."

"You do if you belong to me," he said.

When his mother greeted her at the door, she said, "Joey

good clean boy. Not ner-vous. Me pray for you when my son he be a priest."

"My mother, she's a little soft in the head," Joey explained, and he kissed the old woman, who wasn't very old, and asked her what was to eat.

Joey's mother scurried into the kitchen and pulled from the icebox a lump of sausage as big as your head and half a dozen steaks, a mountain of *polenta* and a gallon of wine. Joey sat down at table with the aloofness of a king. Then his father asked Rita Murphy pointblank:

"What do you want with a punk like my son?" he said.

"Cut it out, Pa," said Joey.

"What's he got, huh? A nice girl like you."

"Pa, will you cut it out!"

"I wouldn't take him on a job. We'd get inside the door, and right away he'd stuff porcelain in the same bag with stoneware. Did you know he tossed a Chinese pot off the bridge because he didn't know what to do with it! His mother wants him to be a priest."

He indicated the woman across the room with the soulful, frightened eyes, who nodded fondly that it was so.

"Nice boy," she said. "Very clean. Make good good priest."

"Did you know he had a box of Roman coins he took to Chicago and sold for weight!"

"Will you cut it out, for Christsake!"

It only made her love him more, because he wasn't a good thief, because his father was so hard. But one morning Joey's mother couldn't get out of bed, and when they stood her on her feet she clattered to the floor like wooden blocks, and two days later she was dead. Then Joey felt that the heart had been cut out of him with a knife, and when the earth opened to welcome his mother, he threw himself down into the pit, and strong men had to draw him out, or he would have been buried there.

After the funeral Joey's father just sat in his chair and stared at the floor, and you could not tell what he thought, except that it was another case of the wicked ways of this world and the faithlessness of women. You would have thought by the way he treated her that that woman meant nothing in his life, but then it was only because he knew all along her faithless ways!

At the other end of the house everyone knew how things stood with Joey, and no one could approach or he would do him harm, and no one could stay away for fear he would injure himself. Marvelous were the maledictions he uttered against himself, and horrible the crimes he confessed to, and no man laid a friendly hand upon his person but he lashed out as he would cleanse the world of such scum, and no woman whispered a kindness in his hearing but she was Slut of Satan and Lucifer's Own Wife.

Rita Murphy saw all this and knew not her place, or what to do, so she went to Joey's father and told him how things stood with his son.

The old man looked at her, and a thought formed in his brain, and he said:

"You, girl. More wine."

He opened his mouth to drink, then paused and told them all to go! Clear out! Vanish! And one by one they filed out of the house, and he went and looked at his son.

"You've known me how many years now that I was a fraud?" he said.

Joey looked at his father and tried to think how long it had been.

"But you," his father said. "I know I ride you—you could do it. I know I put you down—you could be good."

Joey started to speak, but the old man stopped him.

"Maybe it's not right to talk like this with your mother in the ground. I'm not saying I have regrets, but there are reasons things turned out this way. I don't want you to make the same mistake."

He took two glasses and the jug of wine and set them on the table between them.

"You see, if a man wants to do a job of work," he said, "if he's fencing the goods, or planning the heist, or doing his time, it don't make no difference, he wants to do it right, am I wrong? He don't want distractions, because distractions goof him up."

On the table he found ham and bread and cheese, and having discovered his appetite, he commenced to eat.

"Say you got rubies like the last time you had," he said. "You don't want to think all the time how the wife needs bread or the girl friend a fur coat, do you follow me? You want value for value, and maybe you got to run out west to do it right, so the wife thinks you got a girl friend, and the girl friend that you love your wife, do you see how I mean? You got no peace of mind."

He shook his head and frowned at the memory.

"You got a great future in the business," he concluded. "It's up to you."

They were the first kind words his father had said to him, and they sent warm blood through Joey's veins till he felt the urge to stir himself and perform deeds of resolution.

"Don't think of yourself," the old man said, wagging a finger in a forbidding manner. "Think of those few men who are in a position to know and appreciate, and who would know and appreciate that you had joined their number and were one of them. I ain't talking about Capone—a Sicilian bully! Or Frank Dillinger—a figment of the comic books! I'm talking about men you never heard of, like Vito Panelli who stole gas from the pipe line and sold it back to the Arabs. Guys like Numbers Scalasi who bought and sold the same steel back and forth between the Red Chinese and the North Vietnamese and the United States Army so many times that they'd have built him a monument at the Mercantile Exchange if it hadn't all transpired underneath the table. You never heard of these guys because they never got caught. You could be one of them."

He went on to explain how guys like this who really did something didn't live in palaces like kings but lived ascetic, priestly lives devoted to the pursuit of their craft, lives stripped down to racing form like their minds which could penetrate the subtleties and plot the machinations.

"Monks they're like," he said. "But no two-bit penny-ante stuff at the local bank copying out what someone wrote in the book of human deeds. Big time stuff like the Arabs—did you know it's from them we learned to count the loot? And the biggest Arab of all, does he live in a palace with a flock of whores? In the desert he lives with his falcon and his horse. And he thinks big thoughts. But what he plans you can't dream. I could show you how."

A generous impulse sprang into Joey's heart, and he wished to plead with his father that the way to greatness was open to him, too, now that the old woman was dead, but his father raised his hand.

"No," he said, shaking his head and looking away as if he were ashamed. "Certain things . . . impossible. Habits . . . too old."

He blew his nose, and there was a tear in the old crocodile's eye, and his son perceived that the highest mountain is not for the winter of our life, and in a moment of candor he gave his father to know that he, too, had always seen himself as such a one, with such a capability, and indeed there was a third who considered him such, and she. . . .

His father looked at him sadly and wisely, and shook his head.

"A woman?" he said.

Joey nodded.

"Who wants to marry you?" his father said.

Joey held his breath.

"Because she understands?" the old man continued. "Because while you climb the highest mountain she will hold your hand?" He laughed a melancholy laugh and poured his son a little wine. "Those were your mother's words to me," he said. "But are we speaking here of a stroll in the park? Don't you know that those men are the immortals!"

He went on to describe the titanic struggle and the monumental effort which required skill and courage and luck and resolution, and one thing more—self-sacrifice.

"What women want," he said, "is fullness, completeness. Women don't want sacrifice."

What is more natural than that a father should impart to his son the sum of his experience, that he should want his son to be all that he himself is not, or that a husband should blame his wife for the mediocrity of his life, who has stolen him from the bosom of his mother and father and their dream of perfection, and cast him naked into a cruel world!

Joey looked at him and knew that what had kept his father from the pinnacle of greatness was exactly that woman whom he himself had loved as his mother. Still, she had had for him a great and pure thought, and it was his father's thought, too, and the coincidence felt like destiny which he had sensed but never understood until now.

"Tonight," his father said, "the plane to Palermo. I'll explain it to her. Perhaps she'll understand. . . ."

All was done as he said, and Joey was apprenticed to a padrone in the mountains of Sicily, that he might learn the secrets of true theft. This padrone, who never spoke but only gestured with his hand, spent his time hunting with his falcon and watching wild asses breed, and he carried in his boot an ancient stiletto with which he carved up lizards that crept into the light of the cooking fire where he sat at night in contemplation. For three years Joey passed his days in silent attention and his nights in troubled dreams and premonitions, until in the spirit of one seeking solace in talk and the company of human kind, he engaged this padrone in conversation.

Joey told him of his father's hope for him and of his own aspiration, and seeking to display humility in the company of a great man, he said that he found the padrone's ways obscure, and most of all he wished to know what great act he planned.

The padrone thought a long time, and when at last he spoke he said that well he understood himself to be the great man whom Joey had described, and as for his plan it was not obscure at all but accorded with his own father's wish for him to become in his lifetime all that the old man was not, and for this reason he had come into the mountains while his father remained in town where idleness and luxury made a man effeminate, and here in this place in watching wild asses breed and torturing lizards, he went about his father's business.

"What business?" Joey asked, growing bolder each minute

as his conviction grew that what sat before him was not a great man but a fool, for there is nothing like silence to ennoble a man, and nothing like words to bring him down.

"Why, the business that you see," the padrone said, gesturing towards the darkness and breathing in the pure night air. "Why, this perfection."

Joey knew full well the business that lay around them—hadn't he gazed at it every day till its perfect emptiness had blinded him! Rock and wind and blazing light lay around them. Night and dark and a thousand frozen stars.

A bad thought entered his heart, and there grew a desire to leave that place and to come again into his father's presence, and when at last he did return, he went not to his father's house but to the bank, and asked for Banker Murphy.

The girl directed him to the highest floor and down the corridor to the last door, which was marked President, and there behind the desk, a big cigar in his fat jeweled hand, sat Joey's father.

If the son knew his father, the father did not at once know his son, and indeed when Joey saw his own reflection in the polished surface of his father's desk he thought he had changed places with a monkey. His face was black, his skin leather, and his arms where had hung the muscles of his youth were now all wire and rope, and he seized his father by the throat, saying to him in a great voice:

"You tricked me, and married my girl, and stole her wealth, and all these years I have lived like a slave doing another man's work, but now I am returned!"

His father's eyes bulged in his head, and he had about him an odor of decay, or perhaps it was perfume, and when Joey perceived this, he laughed out in surprise and revulsion and let go his father's throat.

The old man called him Son and Noble Youth, swore he had done it all only for Joey's education, and begged his mercy. Joey, his mind unclouded by any human sentiment from living all those years with lizard and falcon and ass, knew his father for the crocodile he was—when in the door came a beautiful, matronly woman who wore on her face the soul of womanly pleasure, and behind her an army of kids.

In a loud voice she denounced his father, calling him Ox and Idiot for having kept her waiting for her lunch, and she didn't care a fig for meetings of the board, she said, and didn't he know she had to be at the hairdresser's! Here she stopped and, eyeing Joey, announced that even beggars were more handsome than bankers these days, and she turned on her heel, leaving behind her the brats in sailor's suits and pinafores who crawled all over their father's desk.

Joey caught up with her in the hall and seized her arm.

"What, am I mad!" cried Rita Murphy, throwing off his hand. "As a thief of diamonds and rubies and banker's daughters, you were a child, and I was a child. But I am a child no longer, and my head is no longer full of childish things. In my life I require something more."

Then she asked where he had been for three years, and he told her about the padrone and the wild asses in the mountains of Sicily, and she laughed until her sides split.

"Three years it has taken you to wake up," she said, "and now you must go into the world."

"You will come with me," Joey said, "because I am young and strong, and he is old and fat. Because my brain is clear, and his—"

She said she would go nowhere but would just as soon stay put. Just because she spoke harshly to his father didn't mean she didn't love him, she said, and that was what Joey must learn, that all these years his father had loved him, too, and even if he hadn't, he had taught him of the double-edgedness of things, and most especially of love, which burns where it is most true. What Joey called woman's faithlessness was really life, she said, and a dramatic privilege to be all that a person could. . . .

It left Joey speechless. So Rita Murphy told him never to think himself a better thief than his father but to go into the world and seek the spirit of manly delight. And with a broken heart he did.

The Popcorn Stand

It was the only place for them, down by the lake, behind the popcorn stand. Not that they ate popcorn, although now and then one would stroll over to the window and come back with a cup of coffee black, but winter and summer there they were, standing on the grass out behind, toying with a ball between them or huddled around the only park bench, playing cards.

Long after the place had closed and it was too dark to see, if you drove by, there would still be a few glowing cigarettes where they always sat, and if you drove past on a Sunday morning on your way home from Chicago or to the airport, when the world was gray and misty down along the lake, two or three of them would be at the table, or perhaps standing in a knot putting down one foot and then the other to keep their shoes dry, and you would think to yourself as you drove past, there go those Serbs. George and Dusan, Robert and Milan and Ibo—it happened to be true that they were Serbian.

In summer the muddy little parking lot was full of the cars and vans and motorcycles of people who had come to eat at the popcorn stand or to go to the beach across the street, but those Serbs never paid attention unless some girl happened to stroll over their way; and down the beach when there was a rock concert on Saturday nights near the place where the old Germans sunbathed and fed the goat on the other side of the private fence, the Serbs who never took off their coats never heard the blare of sound but rather some other music more rapid and insistent which made the ball skip between their feet and set their toes underneath the table to dancing.

You would think they had no other place to go, but George had a nice little bungalow on the west side of town and a wife and two kids, and Milan rented a room from him, the best in the house, George said, but they never said boo to each other there, and each morning they drove down to the lake front before work or after work, and sometimes in the summer they laid off work altogether just to spend more time there. The others were like that, too, Lubic and Dusan and Robert, and at one time or another all had accommodations of perfect respectability, though not always did they have that for long, wives and children, houses and cars and suits of clothes, but rich or poor, married or not, there to the lake front they went and there by the popcorn stand they passed their time.

Of course, there were hundreds of Serbs in that town living lives of the utmost respectability, lawyers and house painters, sellers of automobiles and owners of restaurants, who attended Saint Ivo's on Sunday dressed in their finest suits, accompanied by their wives who might be wearing as much as a pound and a half of gold upon their persons, and their children in finest linen; who listened to the sermon and heard the mass and stayed on at the church all day for the soccer game and the lamb roast and in the evening, while the kids ran themselves to exhaustion about the great hall, for a drink of brandy and a cup of coffee black. Nor was Sunday the only day for going out. For Sunday was a family day and a day of worship, but Saturday you could find them at the SV Lounge or at the Bosniad where the Beo played and you could dance *kolos* till your feet fell off. Wednesdays and Fridays it was the same, and any other day you could spend a quiet evening at Nikki's or Nine Brothers' or Lubic's where the women still cooked on stoves as big as a room and where the kitchen was bigger than the restaurant and had more people in it, too, even when that place out there was full, because they were the kinds of places where everything went to make it right, and if it took five women to serve one customer, so be it. If you went to one of those places you would think that every Serb in town followed that routine, and you would know, too, that it was a routine not of boredom but of decorum, where each thing had its place, from the red wine to the brandy, from the priest's song to the music of the Beo. And these Serbs, George and Milan, Dusan and Ibo and Lubic and the rest about whom I am speaking, followed this routine, too, but always after each event there was the lake front and the popcorn stand.

They were like a generation of them, that gang, and although some were old and some young, all thought of themselves as the same age, and that was because they were the generation born in the mountains of Bosnia and living out there on the west side of that middle western town utterly indistinguishable from any other middle western town except in that it was on the shores of a Great Lake, a lake you can't see across, and to that fact they clung because it suggested to them all they missed and hoped for. The younger ones who were born here never missed anything, and the older ones no longer had hope except for the things of this world, but these were the generation in between, the men of whom I am speaking, and some of them played in that soccer game on Sundays, and some had grown too old to play, but after that game they congregated by the popcorn stand, and then you would see soccer the way it ought to be played on into the twilight, silently and intensely so that the only sound was of strain and of running and of the thump of the ball.

On Dusan's name day his wife prepared a lamb and a pig both, and all sat in the yard drinking wine and brandy, because Dusan had a house by the river then, and the food was the best in all the world and the company, too, everyone agreed; still the men were anxious to go home, and first they dropped off their wives and then drove down to the lake, and though Milan had the cards they did not play, did not talk much either, not even when Dusan himself arrived, for he had just gone out for a drive to settle his stomach after the day and the party, he said, for always a little drive did that for him, and by the time they got home to their wives, those of them that had wives, the women were asleep.

It was a man's world down there, and although some of them had met their wives there, American girls who had drifted over from the beach, drawn by the sight of tall, straight, dark young men, once they married them their wives no longer returned to the beach and the popcorn stand, or if they did and you saw them there you would think they were no more to their husbands than the passing wind. And one husband might come over to his wife to borrow a cigarette or to ask if she had remembered to iron his handkerchief, but that was all; and if one was getting married they all went first to the wedding and reception and afterwards to the popcorn stand, and if one was divorced or thrown out of the house the first place he went was there. When Black Ibo shot the grocery clerk by accident because the fellow had slammed the cash drawer on his fingers, Black Ibo cried, "What for'd you do that!" and the guy bled to death right there in front of him, and the police caught Black Ibo because he went to the popcorn stand. When Dusan got out of jail where he had gone for non-support following his divorce, the first place he went was not his mother's house but there. When George came home and found his wife in Milan's room and swore he would cut out Milan's tripes like a sheep's belly and had the knife in his hand to do it, and he would have done it, too, if

Milan hadn't had the gun in readiness between the mattress and the box spring, and he must have had it there against just such a chance, for his hand went to it more quickly than Nancy, George's wife, could get out of the room, and they faced each other while Milan backed out the door and ran to his car, and still the place he drove was there, and when George followed him and they met, neither spoke to the other in the darkness around that table while the men watched, so many glowing cigarette ends, and then Dusan told the story of what it had been like in prison and how the thing he had missed was to look at water.

"Not cigarettes?" one said.

"My mother brought them."

"Not brandy?"

"That, too. In her thermos."

"Not women?"

Dusan didn't have to answer that, for hadn't a woman sent him there when she signed that paper putting his soul in the hands of the court!

Later they played cards with the flashlight lying on the table lighting up their fingers, the rough boards, the luminous faces of the cards with their little hearts and diamonds, spades and clubs, the colorful embroglio of Jack and King and Queen.

"I bet two."

"Make mine three."

Their voices were grave and serene, while across the road the waves murmured lonely, melancholy words they all understood. And if George and Milan had met in any other place in this world they would have committed murder, each one without a thought, for everyone heard how Milan had had to flee in the night without a stitch of clothing, and how George had beaten his wife with a shoe till she didn't come out of her house for a month except to go to six o'clock Mass, but still there along the lake shore by the popcorn stand nothing had changed.

That was the way it was. Some things could change, but some things remained the same. That was the way it had to be. On the street Ibo laughed at Dusan because Dusan had done time for non-support and Ibo hadn't, even though that grocery clerk had bled to death through the hole in his heart. For Ibo had become one of Big Frankie Melon's bodyguards, and that was how he got off the hook, while Dusan had let a woman do that to him. And if you asked Ibo what a woman was, he could tell you in language that would make your ears burn. Dusan on the street laughed at Ibo just as hard because everyone had heard how Ibo had wept tears over the body of that grocery clerk, begging and pleading with him, shaking him by the shoulder to wake up and live a little—just like a woman he had cried, Dusan said. Still, if women were weak and life was hard, at the popcorn stand by the lake front they were all brothers, and nothing had changed.

If the Bosniad closed its doors for good after two brothers one Saturday night shot Rocco the owner dead, and not because his drinks were overpriced as everyone agreed they were and had to be for the simple reason that the dancers never drank more than one drink and would let that glass sit all night on the table while they danced, and not because he watered his whiskey as everyone agreed he did and had to do for the simple reason that strong whiskey made the dancers sweat, but because of some old quarrel that went back to 1945 and what had happened in another country in another world in the mountains of Bosnia between their fathers or uncles or great-grandfathers—no one knew except that Rocco was dead and the Bosniad closed for good—but still there was that place by the lake front, behind the popcorn stand.

Then Lubic sold his restaurant to his brother-in-law Roberto, and moved back to the old country a rich man, so rich that it made his brother-in-law choke with envy and bite his tongue to keep from telling everyone how Lubic had cheated him at the closing of the deal, and he tried to make it all back in the first month and raised the price of the food and fired the cook and hired a kid who knew no more how to cook than does a rabbit, and Roberto no longer let the customers wander back into the kitchen amidst the polished enamel surfaces of stove and oven to taste this and that and order what suited the tooth since he had let go the old woman whose business it was to polish and prepare and clean, so that Lubic's became no place to go, but still there was the popcorn stand.

At the popcorn stand you were brothers, and you understood each other the way brothers do, even when they pretend they don't, for aren't brothers of the same flesh, and haven't they sprung from the same soil? And if that little seed is torn from the earth before its time and is taken to another world where it knows no one and is left to grow, does it not grow with sorrow in its heart for all it never knew and lost? Even if you quarrel with your brother over the time of day and every little thing about which there should be no quarreling, still he is your brother and he knows. So no matter what they said on the street, at the popcorn stand Ibo could tell Dusan how he had to pack a gun now all the time because Big Frankie had said all his boys had to pack the heat, and how was he to know when they had approached him for the job and told him all the pussy he would get and the fancy clothes, all the fast cars and the respect—how was he to know he'd have to carry a gun? And it wasn't even the gun he minded, it was that where were the fancy clothes and the fast cars, where was the pussy, and it wasn't even that these things weren't there, because they were, it was just that what did they matter when you were afraid? He had thought the gun would mean respect, and it did, but what was respect when you were afraid? There wasn't even much you could do with a woman then.

Dusan didn't laugh because Dusan had had his dreams, too, and what mother's son of them hadn't, as any man does who is born tall and straight and dark, who is made as fine as God can make him! And what did that making cost that it had to be paid for for a lifetime! No, you were sired in contempt, an afternoon or a morning's fling in the long life of your father's disappointment, and what did she who was your mother get for those few moments besides birth pain and heartache and early death, to say nothing of the anger of her son whom she had betrayed to this life of pain and grief. That was what they knew, those brothers there, and that was why they were silent for the most part or idle in their talk despite the fast gay words they flung about town and on the street and at Saint Ivo's, at Nikki's or the SV Lounge, because there were no words to express it. That was why, too, despite their wives and their daughters, their presents on Mother's Day and their following the young skirts, they had contempt for the female kind. For as the world is fickle and as it changes its face every morning, so the world was a woman, and that was what they knew there at the lake shore behind the popcorn stand . . .

One day in December when it rained on the snow that had fallen the day before and they all stood on the edge of concrete by the warmth of the exhaust fan to keep their shoes dry, a woman came to the window of the popcorn stand with a notebook and a pad of paper. No one had come all that day, because of the weather, but this woman had not come to buy popcorn, and they all heard the loudness of Sam the owner's cursing as he told her in no uncertain terms where she could go and what she could do when she got there. Then he stuck his head out the window and jerked his thumb in the direction of Dusan and George and Roberto, and said:

"Tell it to them!"

He slammed the window down, came out the door, and drove away in his car. The woman walked over to where they stood underneath the eave.

"I'm with the city," she said. "The bureau of relocation."

She was not an unattractive woman, although, what with her raincoat and her unaffected manner, they did not see this right away, but gradually it came to them, and so it took them even longer to realize that what she was talking about was the destruction of the place known as the popcorn stand. For if the county had once owned the land upon which it stood, now the city owned it, and while it was all right to lease space for such an establishment from the county, when it became a city matter bids had to be taken and no favoritism shown, even though the whole reason for the city's purchase from the county had to do with the wife of one of the aldermen taking offense at the unsightliness of the place, or perhaps it was that her brother had the little drive-in down the road that wasn't doing so well and he resented the competition, and so the county had been persuaded to sell and the city to buy and the place was to be turned into a duck pond, with no favoritism shown except perhaps in the letting of the contracts to fill and grade. All of this she explained to them with such gravity and intelligence and detachment that they invited her over to the table with them, forgetting the rain that fell on their heads and the snow through which they had to wade, and when they reached the table they said, "Now tell us. Tell us again."

So she did, and at first they wondered, did she know the meaning of what she said, and so they listened a little more and decided that she did, and then they wondered, how could she know the meaning of it, this woman from the city with eyes so dark and mouth so red, and yet explain it all with such detachment—the way a man would explain it! The way they would explain it themselves if they were in their best form and it were their thing to explain!

"What do you think," she said, "you're the first ones who ever lost a building?"

So she told them how the Italians not long ago had had their whole quarter destroyed by the bulldozer and their church torn down; how the Poles had had a freeway carved through the heart of their quarter and one house set apart from its neighbor by a gulf of roaring traffic and a lot of cyclone fence till those neighbors could not hear themselves think; and how the blacks had had their quarter carved up by highways and urban renewal and everything the mind of man could dream of till block upon block of it was a wasteland of stones and broken bottles and old bricks where not even peas would grow—all of which those young men listened to with perfect complacency.

"But that's the Italians," one said. "That's the Negroes and the Poles."

Still they wondered in their hearts, what did those people do?

"They had to relocate," she said.

Relocate, they thought to themselves. They did not know for certain that they had ever in their lives heard that word. What could be its meaning?

"You see, those Italians come from Italy," one said.

"Poles come from Poland," said another, gesturing with his hand to explain these matters of geography, of fate and destiny and the way of the world, to this grave young woman who wore no gold upon her person when she went out of the house, who when she spoke did not smile or blink her eyes or lose her temper, and to express to her how natural it was that Poles or Italians should find their worlds shattered and their lives thrown into the whirlwind. For hadn't Italy been overrun by Greeks and Trojans and Carthaginians since time out of mind? Hadn't the same happened to the Poles by way of Russia or Finland or Germany or wherever? That was what happened to people's houses where they lived.

"The others come from Alabama," Milan said.

"But from Africa," George added.

They nodded. It was a further instance of the common destiny of men who lived as nations or tribes, in houses. And she listened, for she had never heard matters explained in this way, and it occurred to her that there were facts about this world she had yet to learn, and that these dark men who were so tall and straight, who moved through the snow with such lightness, shod in black leather, were the ones to explain it.

"And you?" she said. "Where do you come from?"

"We?" said Dusan. He looked at the others with a short laugh, and gestured towards the bleak winterscape of wet snow and shiny black trees, of parking lot and glistening street, beyond which the water rose up in a sluggish undulation, underneath a leaden sky. "We come from here."

They nodded to each other and smiled with satisfaction that one of their kind could express what all felt in their hearts, that in truth they were children of nowhere so much as of there, that they had found a way to endure the changes of this mutable world by embracing not the past which they had been too young really to know, and not the present where they had so little control, and not the future which they learned each day a little more not to believe in, and certainly not houses and tribes and nations and families and wives and children, but this place here, the popcorn stand. And they were like philosophers who, setting their minds on the unattainable high thing which is not of this world, never confuse Beauty with the pretty little things of this earth, nor Truth with the sharpness of this world's reality which changes as the wind, nor Goodness with their own pleasure, and so they did not believe in the rewards of this world and instead contented themselves with lowly things which might survive and endure, like the popcorn stand.

"Are you married?" she asked.

They looked at one another and decided that they were, whether that was a laughing matter or not, but what did it have to do with anything? Weren't their wives just the opposite of themselves, setting their thoughts always upon the world's gold and the world's truth and most of all upon their own pleasure?

"But if she sets her mind upon the beauties of this world," she said, this woman from the city, the bureau of relocation, "isn't it only to make herself more pleasing to her husband, and to console him in his quest for the unattainable high thing?"

They looked at one another and shrugged. It could be that what she said was so, but what did it matter, since when one reached a certain age one was no longer pleased or consoled?

"But if she sets her mind upon the world's truth," said this woman from the city, "and speaks harsh words about this world's reality, isn't it only to help her mate steer his course through the perilous seas while he keeps his eye fixed upon the high thing, and to help him keep his feet free from the many low encumbrances along the way?"

They exchanged a glance and a frown. For never had they heard a woman speak like this, so like a man, and never had they heard matters explained this way, as if they and their wives were sharers of a common destiny and the true pathos of the human situation.

"And if they set their minds upon their own pleasure," she

continued, "isn't it only to make life a little less disagreeable for those around them and to help all bear the burdens of the world, in which all suffer, with grace and dignity and an even temper?"

For some time after she had finished speaking, all sat around that table in silence. The rain had turned back into snow. No one was sure just what this young woman had said, who was so grave and who spoke with such passionate detachment, nor where she had learned the words, whether in school, or were they written down in some book? But all agreed the words were good, well chosen and in every way worthy of their feelings about themselves and this place where they sat; and yet her words had represented their wives as one of themselves, as they themselves were, not perhaps in reality but rather in their dreams and ideal conceptions, for what one of them did not know in his heart how short he sometimes came of his own ideal conception, for that was a human thing, that shortfall, and yet this woman had represented their wives in that light, too, as one of them, as worthy of a place at that table behind the popcorn stand.

Perhaps it was a thought like this, or perhaps it was a drop of water that found its way down George's neck, but he sat up and shook himself like a wet dog, and looked around, and wondered what he was doing sitting there in the rain. Never in all his life had such a question occurred to him, and perhaps for the first time he saw that snug little bungalow on the west side of town and a fire on the hearth and a glass of brandy and a cup of coffee black, but he got up and went to his car, and one by one they all drifted over that way, each bound up in his own thoughts, and drove away.

That woman, too, went to her car and wrote words in her notebook. I don't know what words she wrote, but the next day a bulldozer and a dump truck came, and first they pushed that popcorn stand over on her side until she was a heap of kindling, and then they loaded her on that truck. The next day the city came with rolls of snow fence and a no-parking sign and fenced off that parking lot and posted the boulevard, and I don't know whether those Serbs found some other place in this world or whether they just stayed home with their wives, but when you drive down along the beach now you see people sunbathing and listening to music and feeding the goat or the ducks, but those Serbs and their popcorn stand are gone.

The Masculine Principle

FOR fifteen years Joe Harriot never had a problem with his father-in-law, and then it wasn't his so much as his wife's. It started with the new dog. Everyone agreed there should be no new dog once Pontifex died, but no sooner had Pontifex done so than John Porteous came home with a puppy from the Pound.

Evie and her mother looked at each other, but no one said a word, of course, and it was a fresh little thing with eyes the color of wet terra cotta and feet ten times too big. Pontifex had been old so long, and usually he just slept in the chair, so that you forgot what dogs were like. Of course, he'd had his difficulties, and if you tried to move him he growled and bared his teeth, but this puppy just didn't sit still, and every time Evie's mother was away to the store, John Porteous called his daughter.

He called at all hours, at four in the morning, at ten at night, and Joe would wake up to find his wife getting dressed.

"Mother's in Chicago," she said, "and the dog won't let him sleep."

"What can you do?"

"Boil him an egg, and take him for a walk."

"Your father, or the dog?"

The next time her mother went away, the old man wanted Evie to stay the night.

"Do you think I want to go?" she said.

"He should get rid of the thing, if he can't take care of it."

"I'll talk to him. He's just a puppy."

Her father was a man of sixty-seven, he reminded her, and if the dog was pampered now, he wasn't likely to improve with age.

Indeed, he just got bigger. When you walked in the door, instead of having him up on your legs, he jumped up on your stomach and licked your hand, and it wasn't long before he threw his paws on your shoulders and washed your face with his tongue. Of course, he was the best natured dog in the world, but on his hind legs he was taller than half the women who entered the house, and it was more than most of them could take, a hundred-forty-pound dog looking at them with his terra cotta eyes, breathing hotly and wetly in their faces.

The funny thing was that Evie's father liked it. It wasn't that he encouraged the beast, and in fact he always sprang to his guest's defense, beating with a rolled-up newspaper upon the dog's rump, who took it for a great game, and barked and romped, so that everyone entering the house came in to general confusion not unmarked by the threat of being toppled over, flogged with that rope of a tail, and trampled under elephant feet.

He was tall and shaggy, with a great head and jaws like an Irish wolfhound, and John Porteous had read in a book that the wolfhound, though he had accompanied Harald Hardrada to Constantinople and overthrown the Turk, was of a gentle, affectionate nature, and nothing would convince him differently about his Rigel. That was what he called him, after the giant star in the foot of Orion.

"Your father's mad," Joe Harriot said one evening at dinner.

But Evie had a way of seeing a thing in its proper light.

"It's those people who visit my mother," she said. "He's fed up with them. I'd like to see you put up with it."

She made it sound as if she were on the dog's side.

"I thought you liked your mother's friends," he said. "I thought they were your father's friends, too."

Oh, she did, she said. And they were. He was just "fed up."

Guests had been one of the things the Porteous house was known for. Guests for the weekend. Guests for dinner. Guests from Chicago for the Monday-night concerts. Guests the next morning for breakfast. . . . There was no end of guests, all of them old friends, all of them staying a little longer, all of them perfectly charming and civilized, so that the house rang with music and laughter and reasonable talk, with the sound of crystal and of fine cutlery, with discussions of Galileo and Thomas Jefferson and Bach. When it became clear that Rigel was going to change all this, the old friends called Evie.

She had to talk with her father, they said. The dog was destroying the house. Why, just last weekend with his tail he had cleared a table of a Chinese porcelain, a "priceless piece of your father's collection." And when they knew by the vagueness of her response that they hadn't hit home, they reminded her that such things as the Chinese vase would have gone to her, if they hadn't gone into the garbage. When they knew again that they hadn't found her, they said the house smelled of dog.

It was true, too. The house stank. Long scoriations marked the front door, and the glass was out on the porch and in two of the living room windows where Rigel had simply lunged through. There was no end of broken and discarded objects which the beast with his tail had swept to the floor, so that the place seemed empty compared with its former elegant clutter. The Oriental he had chewed beyond repair, the table clock he tipped and smashed . . . but the telling thing, to Joe Harriot's mind, was the smell.

You walked in the door, and on a hot day in summer it made you catch your breath. The house had the pungency of a cattlebarn, and you wondered how they could take it, until you realized that Evie's mother didn't even know, and that her father—but he watched you, gauged your response in accordance with some theory he had, some test. . . . It was the strangest thing in the world. That was why Evie never spoke to him, in spite of telling everyone that she would. Her mother? Well, Rigel was a big baby whom she loved and coddled and understood, an orphan she had taken in, an abandoned child. But her father? Her father was going through something, Evie said. It weighed on her mind.

"My father doesn't believe in things anymore," she told her husband.

"What things?" The notion shocked Joe Harriot. "Do you mean music and drama? Do you mean old clocks?"

"He doesn't believe in anything," she said.

"What about friends? What about you and your mother?"

She didn't answer, just shook her head.

"Did you know that 'Rigel' means foot?" she said. "I looked it up in my father's book."

"He believes in his dog, you mean."

"He believes in his foot."

He could think only of giving people the boot, kicking things to pieces, and on the contrary Rigel was the friendliest, most affectionate creature you could imagine. He greeted everyone with open arms and slobbering good cheer. When he panted he grinned at you. He had a good laugh. And John Porteous stood back and watched with certain pleasure. Still, to Evie he believed in nothing save his dog—his foot.

The real trials came at dinner, for if the dog was excluded he set up such a howling, clawing protest on the other side of the kitchen door that conversation was impossible, and the table sat in silence, or dissolved in laughter until someone rose to let the creature in. Then, of course, he had to be fed with everyone else, with peas and squash and lettuce, with okra and aubergine and all manner of good things, or else he would wrestle with a bone on the floor as if it were a rat, tossing it in the air, till he dominated the meal so completely that it left off being a time of taste and good talk and became a tribute to raw, exuberant appetite.

If Evie's father carved the roast, there was the dog with his head above the table, and his nose under John Porteous's arm, and all eyes watched to see how close that nose came to the carved portion, and not infrequently the tongue licked out, which brought a murmur from his master, a protest completely ineffectual, and nothing more.

In this manner a dozen slices of the roast might be marked by the creature for himself alone, and all eyes watched to see if any of these made its way on to a passed plate. Too often after the beast had marked out his own, there was barely enough to go around, so that at that meal one appetite and one alone was served. Then one evening when the conversation turned, as it so often did, from Vivaldi and things musical to Thomas Jefferson and the drafters of the American Declaration, John Porteous leaned across the table and in a confidential tone whispered to his son-in-law:

"I am a man who has eaten the flesh of a woolly mammoth."

All eyes turned, and Rigel looked at them, blinking sleepily, while John Porteous picked up his knife and fork and returned to his plate, one corner of which the dog had washed clean.

It was true, Evie told him later. Everyone knew the story; that was why no one was surprised. The remains of the prehistoric creature had been found in the ice in Siberia in such a state of preservation that a side of meat had been flown to New York, where Charles at the Waldorf prepared it for the Explorer's Club. Everyone knew the story.

They may have known it, Joe Harriot thought, but until they met Rigel they had never seen the thing in its proper light. . . .

One of Evie's father's oldest friends was Professor Eliot from the University, with whom he had used to sit up half the night arguing the American Revolution, and when Eliot had written his book, he had dedicated it to his friend. It was well known they disagreed, and that had been the spirit of the dedication, too, for Eliot held with the American Loyalists for whom the Revolution was wrong-headed, its ideals simple-minded and naive, and in his book he attributed the difficulties of our present age to just this "dangerous innocence," to which, in his opinion, his friend had long subscribed. The first time Eliot came to dinner "in the year of that dog" he didn't wait past eight the next morning before he called Evie.

He reminded her that, as her godfather, he had taught her her Lord's Prayer and her Creed, and had always thought of her with great affection, but "since that dog" her father had gone too far. What the dog had done, in Professor Eliot's estimation, was to alter her father's opinion in a way that Professor Eliot himself had been unable to do: Rigel had convinced him, first, of the naiveté of our Founding Fathers' view of the nature of things as expressed in their Declaration, and second, of how completely we must forego "all Anglo-Saxon restraint" and give ourselves over to appetite.

"Cynicism!" Professor Eliot proclaimed. "He's giving in to the old world's hereditary wrong!"

On the subject Evie's father had nothing to say. But if old Eliot ceased coming to the house "as long as he entertains the brute," John Porteous could sit up half the night with Curly and Jack, two truckers who professed an interest in astrology and who had bought a telescope to study the habits of Venus and Mercury and Mars. That was the reason for the purchase, they said, but judging from the raucous laughter in the upstairs study, they kept it trained instead on the neighbor's bedroom window. Then the dog got out and was gone two days "chasing that Setter bitch up the block."

"Better than having him hump every man, woman, and child who knocks on the front door," Evie said.

For Curly and Jack her father kept the ice box full of beer. But one day when Evie was "sitting for the dog," Curly arrived a little early and chased her around the dining room table until her parents came home.

Her mother would have done murder on the spot, but her father ushered Curly upstairs, and over his shoulder thanked Evie for the sitting, then paused before he ascended any farther. There was no need to worry, he explained confidentially. "Curly's had the mumps. . . ."

It was one of those long luxurious summer evenings, and as she walked up the street, it occurred to her that they had the telescope trained on the panels of her skirt, and did her ears deceive her, or was the house back there full of catcalls and raucous, male laughter?

"It doesn't happen every day," she said to Joe, by way of making him see the thing in its proper light, as something highly unusual.

"And suppose Curly'd caught you!" he said. "He would have, if he hadn't had the mumps!"

"If he hadn't had the mumps he wouldn't try. You're mad because it's my father."

"He acts like some teenage kid!"

"He doesn't have to act like a father all the time, does he? I mean, to hell with clocks and pots and old friends! To hell with decorum and good taste and responsibility! What's life all about, anyhow!"

"Then why do you look so sad?"

"It doesn't happen every day, that's all," she said. "It means I'm a woman of a certain age."

He saw her mother, too, in the instant, and why the dog didn't upset her, why they could be said positively to love the brute. It was the masculine principle they loved, the scent of it in the house. Still, you couldn't have it assaulting your wife, not in the form of a great black dog any more than in the person of Curly. The thought raised hackles on Joe Harriot's back, and sent him that Saturday afternoon to his father-in-law's door.

Evie's mother answered, not to his knock but to the bellowing uproar inside, which was enough to make a grown man look to the strength of hinges and stand light upon his feet.

"Oh, it's you, Joe," she said, holding the dog off him. But the struggle tickled her funny bone more than anything else, and before Joe had gained the front hall she had given way to her enjoyment of it, except that whether his arrival was an excuse for the dog to hug her, or she the dog, wasn't exactly clear.

"Look at you, you oaf!" she cried, affecting impatience with him. "Oh, you no-good ox! Behave, lummox!"

Indeed, she no more hugged him than Rigel collapsed on the floor, spreading his legs to have his belly rubbed, which despite her feigned exasperation she did with glee. It was all too infuriating. It made Joe Harriot want to beat someone with his fists. Would she coddle the brute! Would she keep cold beer for him in the icebox!

"Look at you, fool!" she cried. "Oh, Rigel, you devil, you. Oh, you great black hairy devil!"

Something of the temper Joe was in came through to her at last, for one glance at his face and she went red as a brick and left the room, saying she'd make tea and that her husband would be down in a minute.

At once the dog scrambled to his feet and made to spring on Joe, and just as suddenly Joe glared at him, and the dog froze. Again he made to jump, with great wagging of his tail as if to say, "When does the fun begin?" but Joe curled back his lip and growled in earnest, and Rigel let out a yelp and disappeared under the piano.

The yelp so startled Joe that he thought he had trod on the dog's tail. He listened to the house, and it was ungodly silent. He peered under the piano, and the dog darted out the other side and slithered under the couch, making a high-pitched whimpering that sent panic down Joe Harriot's spine.

"Rigel," he said in a strained whisper. "Good boy, Rigel. Come out."

He stepped towards the couch and bent down to look under, and Rigel bolted out the side, straight through the end table, wearing it like a collar, scattering the books and upsetting the lamp, and disappeared, his tail between his legs, behind the clock.

He was trying to make it to the hall, and Joe stepped aside to let him have his way, before he realized how awful it would be if the dog reached the kitchen in that craven posture. He imagined his in-laws' outrage and astonishment as they saw their son-in-law for the bully that he was: It was bad enough he had stolen their only daughter, but what had he done to their Rigel, their baby?

"Rigel, please," he pleaded. "For godsake, it's all right."

The clock trembled and swayed, and he didn't know if he should run to it, and then the clock tipped, and he lunged to catch it, and the dog bolted past him through the door, howling as if he'd been murdered.

"What in heaven's name!"

John Porteous appeared behind him, lifting the clock off Joe's shoulder where he'd caught it, and behind him stood Evie's mother with the tea.

"Damned brute!" John Porteous said. "How on earth did you catch it, Joe? Thank God for that! The damned beast!"

Joe's knees felt weak enough that he was thankful to sit down.

"And the books!" the old man cried, on his hands and knees by the end table pawing through the mess. "Why did you get in the books, Rigel? Do you think you can read? Then you'll want to know the reason why!"

They were all three of them, somehow, terribly excited, and as Rigel peered around the kitchen door, it took nothing less than a chorus of pampering, cajoling, affectionate praises to bring him sheepishly into the room, and nothing less than Joe Harriot patting his head, and finally, when he had collapsed on his back on the floor and looked up at them with his great, lost, wet, alien eyes, nothing less than Joe rubbing his belly, to restore him to anything like his former self.

"The damn dog's got a conscience," John Porteous said in amazement and disgust.

"Look at you, you poor fool," his wife cooed. "Oh, I love you so much. Look at you, you great ape, you'll just have to grow up and live in a house."

It was the masculine principle, all right. Rigel looked at Joe, and they both knew.

Voyages

SOME women are not really women at all, but pirates. The same goes for men—not that they're pirates but that they aren't men.

The truth about men dawned on me when I married; the truth about women not till later. What is a man, you would have asked me then, and phrases such as "forthright and courageous," "capable but gentle," would have sprung from my lips. A few weeks of living with my wife revealed that I was none of these but rather a creature of furtive moods and fiery temperament, and violence, matched by sheer cowardice and abject funk.

I was not always that way, and in fact before my wedding I was carefree and easy going. I drank too much and opened my mouth to express the simplicity of my heart. But God gave me imagination, too, and a little reflection upon the ways of this world and my situation in it showed me where such behavior would lead.

I have since become a reasonable person, orderly in my habits, responsible and careful as I must be to live in this world, or long since I would have thrown caution to the wind and signed my life away on some promissory note and ended up in jail. Such would have been not an act of manliness on my part but a failure of nerve, and where scoffers have readily identified manliness with deeds of desperation, as if to say, "What more can you expect from a man!" no one identifies it with orderly habits and mere circumspection, the attributes of a husband.

I have explained to my wife certain facts about this world, and it's not that she doesn't understand when I tell her we can't afford the new house.

"I know, I know," she says, leaning across the table to pour me more wine. "But what the hell, let's take it!"

She means it that way, too, not buy it but take it. Still, I never thought of her as a pirate till one day she asked me for a pencil and I told her they were in my desk, and when I went into my study sometime later I found that our home had been burgled. The drawer was pulled out till it hung precariously, and the strewn contents gave so strongly the impression of violent pillaging that the hairs on the back of my neck stirred and I felt myself in the presence of an outlaw or desperado.

Some moments passed before I realized it was my wife, and even then it seemed she must have stolen the checkbook, rifled the desk for cash, and left me for good. I looked for her through the house and found her in the kitchen.

"Did you find the pencil?" I said.

"Yes."

"Where?"

"In the desk. Why do you look like that?"

She was telling me there was nothing unusual in her ransacking the place for a pencil that was in plain view. It was just her nature.

My wife is not large. The muscle in her arm is as nothing. But I remembered then our early married days and the skill with which she engaged in close, hand-to-hand combat with an adversary of twice her strength and emerged without a scratch. Remembering it, I marveled at her nerve, for the arena of our controversy was no bigger than a double bed, and to be confined there in the dark is a little like lying down with a dragon in his den.

In conversation with my fellows I have learned that such behavior typifies women, although some report their wives go not so far as to spend the night. What could you call a woman who would lie down with a dragon and even fall asleep—what else but a pirate?

When I married my wife I revealed myself a dragon, as is natural, for dragons are furtive, moody creatures, full of cravenness and fire which no human form or childish pretense can conceal. But a pirate is more than a natural phenomenon; a pirate takes a philosophical stance to the world, as do outlaws and desperadoes. Now, there are all kinds of outlaws, just as there are philosophers, and some are cynics, and some sober men who quail at the ticking of a clock, and my wife is none of these. Indeed, I believe that her breed descends from the Titans of old, a race of giants who were overthrown by the gods—Zeus, Hades, Poseidon, and the rest of that gang of vain, conniving, lame, pusillanimous usurpers, who rule with the pretense of reason and exile their enemies to the Caucasus, or hold them in thrall doing the work of a bondsman turning the millstones of this world.

Pirates were questing souls, and only a blind man would give their search and the treasure for which they yearned a wholly material character. They sailed the seas and lived an elemental life, which of old gave rise to the philosophical mind, which society laughs at as impractical and unproductive, and forever tries to thwart and trick with its pretense of order and the rule of law. Not for pirates was the city house and the country house, the station wagon and the sports car, which have gone about as far as they can in gelding the rest of us.

Thus I come home from a day of looking into the practical affairs of men, and find my wife with her feet up on the kitchen table and a finger in her cheek, which betokens thought, and before I ask after the children and the washing machine and whether both are well, she tells me that the sun is cooler than we think, that Jupiter's inner moons harbor life, owing to the intensity of reflected light, and that the civilization of Atlantis lies off the coast of New York, buried under mountains of sludge.

How does she know these things? She has read them in a book. I ask for the name of the book, profess an interest in hearing more. It was a book from the library, she says, props her cheek upon her finger, and gazes out the window.

"Did you know that off the coast of Orkney," she says, "in the Pentland Firth, fishermen sighted a dragon that reared up out of the water a hundred and twenty feet, higher than the mast?"

"Why are you telling me?"

"Your son asked if dragons were real. I thought you might want to know."

"A mast?" I say, to control my panic, for I see that she wishes me to have words of intelligence to report to my son. "Then it must have been an old book!" I cry, to keep from speaking about the breakfast dishes in the sink, or my daughter whom I have found outside with her coat off and her nose running, and when I told her to go in for her jacket, she dashed off down the block claiming she was "boiling."

"No," my wife says, "the book was not old," and gazes out the window.

I speak to her about the dishes and our daughter's nose. She answers that in Nepal the sherpas walk barefoot up the frozen avalanche, that in Scotland schoolboys go to school barelegged all winter, and that outside our window the sun shines and the leaves still cling to the trees.

My wife has never been to Scotland or Nepal, nor to my knowledge to the moons of Jupiter. Her conversation speaks of a vast experience, far beyond my knowledge of who or what she is.

I look at my daughter now and think of the word "boiling." I remember her tear-stained face as she asked me once, in a fury, did I want her to "break up the house?"—a threat so out of proportion with her years and size that I took it as some ancestral longing for havoc, some piratical instinct to hack and slash. I remember my wife in the course of treatment for a dreadful disease which seemed as if it would ravage her body, as it is known to do to humankind, probing the mind and indeed carving away at all the parts until it has satisfied its curiosity as to what makes up the creature—I remember her enduring this as if it were nothing, while grown men and brawny lads trembled and cried, lost their wits and their will to live. But she had come from sterner stock, well used to floggings before the mast, to amputations and brandings without benefit of clergy or medical opinion or the pretense of justice. For nothing is hard to bear if we think we need it.

Still, all the hints of pirate in these women have not to do with violence. I come home from work to discover that my mother-in-law, in the course of walking her large black dog, has stopped by the house to speak words with my wife and that the three of them sit at table drinking tea. They have poured the dog's portion into a bowl which they place on the table, and he sits on a chair between them and slurps. They offer no explanation for this behavior—because to them it is natural.

I have passed many nights in the library studying the behavior of remote tribes and obscure classes of men. In Scotland they feed the dogs under the table and sometimes sleep there together with them afterwards. In Singapore and the islands of the Malay archipelago they eat dogs roasted and stewed, the carcass of a fine specimen dressing the table at a feast. Indians of the great plains sometimes throw a dog that happens by, fur and all, into the pot. But nowhere within the walls of the known world do people drink tea at table with these domestic beasts. What am I to conclude but that it marks the behavior of pirates and desperadoes who live beyond the pales of our life, on the high seas or in their underground robber dens where, for companionship or cheerfulness, dogs are prized above their natural station.

The only hint I have found comes from the pen of a nameless Irish monk, a class of men who plied the waves in tiny leather boats to get to their island retreats and who doubtless kept company with rogues and desperate men. "The dog," he writes, "is the most sagacious of the beasts, for only the dog knows his own name."

These words speak to me of a man who has not only drunk tea but held conversation with a dog. My wife and her mother and daughter, too, descend from like kind, pirates and desperadoes, exiles and outlaws and seafaring monks.

I lie awake at night, and where I had admired her courage, to pass the night beside the sleeping dragon, so now it is myself I marvel at, to lie down beside a pirate. I would call it innocence, except that I have read in a book that pirates never fail to subdue these simple fiery creatures with subtle wit and nifty work with a cutlass. Perhaps it is not my courage, then, but my fatality.

Still, she bears me no ill will. Her sleep is untroubled, if expansive, for she takes up all the bed, and I am left with a narrow portion to one side. Towards morning I doze a little and awake to find her looking at me with one eye.

"For what do you wait?" I whisper, my mind full of a nameless dread.

She does not hear me, or perhaps I have not spoken. Sometimes I wonder if my senses are not askew and if my perception of her as a pirate is not really the hint of something upside down in the history of men. I have read in a book that in the beginning men were the philosophers and dreamers and women the keepers of tents, oxen, and jars of honey. Men named the stars and planted seeds in the garden. Women did the work. It was a spiritual life for men, and for women a patient routine of tidying the tent and counting the honey jars, which served as money and betokened wealth. If an ox was to be bought or sold, the woman handled the affair, for the material world was feminine, like the earth, and the spirit masculine, like light and the sun. If the food was not to the man's tooth he did not raise his hand against his wife, but shook his head and sighed and cared not overmuch for his belly.

Now, whether the gods bred a race of beings exclusively to be man's helpmate, as the bible has it, or whether the men captured a lot of pirates and subdued them by means of witchcraft, my author does not say, but it is clear that at some time between now and then things have fallen into a sorry state, and I suspect that the women stole the book of black art and turned its magic upon their captors.

I cannot think how else my life should have come to resemble that of a caged brute, nor why the affairs of this world and the guardianship of its treasure hordes should preoccupy me entirely. In those moments between sleep and waking when we lie in bed and speak of the things in our hearts, I listen for hints of the magic that holds me in thrall.

"You worry too much," my wife says. "You shouldn't drink coffee."

This I dismiss as advice to a child to beguile his head with sleep.

"Do you think I'm beautiful?" she asks.

She gets up and takes her nightgown off over her head and stands before me, watching my face as if it were a mirror. I think of her illness and the way it probed and then withdrew, leaving no trace, leaving her indeed fresher than before. I wonder if pirates, too, grow new limbs and other organs.

"Well?" she says.

"Yes."

"But I mean beautiful," she says.

"Yes."

"Is that all you can say?—"

Quick as a snake I grab her, and she falls on me heavily and laughs, then crawls back under the covers, puts her finger in her cheek, and stares at the ceiling.

"Yes, beautiful," I say. "Of course, there are dragons in the Pentland Firth, and Atlantis is in the North Atlantic, though farther to the east than your maps indicate, but as to life on the moons of Jupiter, whether or not it's there, it will have nothing to say for quite some time."

"Millions of years," she agrees, giggling. And she squirms in the bed to express her unaccustomed delight.

"As to your mother's dog," I say, "where it may be true that dogs are companionable beasts, wise enough to talk with—"

"Yes?" she says.

"On a voyage such as ours, they do not take their tea at table."

"On a voyage such as ours," she says, turning to me, though without her usual abandon. I have prepared myself for that pirate-like elbow in the ribs, and yet none has come, and there is a sobriety in her that I like. "On a voyage such as ours. Yes. Say no more about it."

And I never did.

Snow

THE natural history part of the museum was just next door to the part on civilization, and when he wanted to show her about the development of the earth's crust and its atmosphere, she dragged him back to armaments and war.

"Look, Dad," she said. "Guns."

They were indeed the more dramatic to a six-year-old, wide-bored handguns from Germany, Spanish sabres and cutlasses, a Norman mace such as the brother of William the Conqueror might have used, the note said, because he was a bishop and, as a bishop, forbidden the use of sword.

Still, he had come to Chicago to show her about stones, about weather. . . . Flora had got interested in some Greek pots, had wandered off, and he hadn't seen her in an hour.

"Do you have a gun, Dad?"

"No."

"Yes, you do. In the closet."

"Oh, that," he said. "Yes."

"Do you shoot people?"

"No."

"But sometimes you do, right?"

"Not very often."

Flora came up behind them as they stood before a diorama on medieval warfare. On foot or horseback the figures were cruel in their expression, wild, amazed, appalled, and he saw his own face and the faces of his wife and daughter superimposed in the reflection on the glass.

"It's still snowing," Flora said.

"How were the pots?"

"I was thinking about that. Did the geometrics come before the octopus design, or is it the other way around? Then there's that woman holding snakes, with her hair down so and her breasts painted blue. I used to have her picture in my bedroom, and I saw her every night."

"Let's get something to eat," he said.

"I think we should go," said Flora. "I'm worried about the snow."

They walked back through the part of the museum on natural history till they came to the diorama of the man riding the woolly mammoth.

"Why is he riding the elephant, Mom?"

"He's making him work for him, dear. The way we make horses and cows."

"But why does he make him?"

"Because he has to, to eat. The note says there were glaciers then, and people were forced towards the equator and had to domesticate wild beasts."

"Can I ride an elephant?"

"Wouldn't it be fun!"

"We don't live where they live."

"Maybe we'll have to go there someday."

"To the zoo?"

"Not the zoo. Where they live."

"Just wild? But will we have to?"

They looked at the shadowy vegetation, at the beast, at the brown-skinned man, his face austere, vaguely smiling.

"If we have glaciers will we have to move, Mom?"

"Maybe," said Flora.

"Why does he laugh?"

"Does he laugh?" said Flora.

"I see his teeth."

There were not answers to everything, and Flora did her best as they sat in the cafeteria over coffee and hot chocolate and ice cream.

"Don't you wish they had a museum," she was saying, "where you could see the things we like to imagine. About elephants and whales. About floods and fires. About people. Oh, I know you couldn't show it in a museum."

"What?" he said.

"The things we do, the things we think, the things we like to dream. It's all about how easy it is to die. It's all about stepping into the river and learning to swim. I mean, you can't hold back. You have to give yourself up to it. But give up too much, and you drown. It's not just dying; it's the indifference—how alone we all are. But knowing you're alone, feeling cut off and sorry for yourself, makes it impossible for anything else."

She looked in the direction of the lobby.

"What's the matter?" he said.

"I think we should go, that's all. If we don't, I think we should stay."

"Over night?"

"Till it's over," she said. "The storm."

The lobby had a vaulted ceiling, and the sound of the crowd reverberated hollowly. Through the lobby, out the glass doors, he saw the snow curl lazily in the shelter of the building. . . .

When they got in the car, the clock on the dash said four. Snow was still falling, and falling hard. Across the bald strip of the museum parking lot, out of the shadow of the building, the wind scoured the frozen crust. He rubbed his hands together and eased the car along, waiting for it to warm. It was much worse than he had imagined.

"You've been thinking about your sister," he said.

Flora's sister and brother-in-law had just moved to Florida in the course of reconciliation following their divorce. They were two bright, attractive, impossible human beings, and Flora had been close to them both.

"Do you think they're all right, then?" he said.

Flora looked at him and frowned.

"What do you mean?" she said. "No, of course not."

They drove through the downtown streets in the direction of the highway. The sky was grey and luminous. There were few cars out, and the buildings they passed had lighted windows. It gave the impression of evening. Jeanie stood on the back seat, leaning forward so that her head was right between her mother's and father's. He glanced at her and then at Flora, and saw her looking ahead at the snow.

"Why shouldn't they be?" he said. "They're back together now. There's no more. . . ."

"There's no more my mother? You think that's all that was the matter, their living here?"

He didn't know what to say. He didn't know if he should go into it.

"He had a family, too, don't forget. But it wasn't any of that. At least let's be honest about it. It was themselves, the willingness to let things go, the reluctance to call a halt. They were like spoiled children, wanting their own way, angry when they didn't get it. It's impossible then."

"But now?" he said. "Why do you say no?"

"No what?"

"That they aren't all right."

"I've known them too long," she said after a moment.

"You've known your sister."

"I've known them both."

They reached the highway and headed north. He was surprised to find the traffic heavy, surprised and pleased. The snow had let up now that he was moving faster, and the cars and trucks threw up with their tires a blur of moisture. The wind was steady, blowing west to east across his path, and far ahead against a windrow of evergreens he saw that the snow had not let up at all.

A semi hurtled past, and the wind belted him.

"What the hell—"

"That's ice," Flora said, and he knew that she had felt it, too.

He glanced at her, and she looked straight ahead, open-mouthed. The semi had become a ghost of itself. He opened his window, and the wind shrieked at the crack, and he closed it again. Jeanie, too, stared out the window, transfixed by the swirling snow.

"How long had you known him?" he said.

"Since I was a girl."

"You never told me that."

"You never asked."

"But how did you know him? How did you meet?"

She did not answer till he asked again. Then she said, "Why does this come up now?"

"I don't know," he said. "You've been so far off today." It was something he had always felt that had made him resent his brother-in-law. It was something in the way she said, since she was a girl.

"Look, is what you really want to know," she said, "whether or not we made love?"

"Yes," he said. "Why do you laugh?"

"Because that's what she wanted to know, too."

"Your sister? Did you know him before she did?"

"And when she found out—"

"You never told me you loved him."

"I don't think I did. We were too much alike—too selfish."

"What was she jealous of?"

"Just that. That we had made love—"

"What makes snow, Mom?" Jeanie said.

"Water," said Flora. "And cold."

"But where does it come from?"

"It just comes."

"Does God make it?"

"Yes," said Flora.

"Why?"

"I don't know."

"I don't like it," said Jeanie. "It scares me."

"Sometimes it's scary," said Flora, "but sometimes it's fun."

The traffic had dispersed. What remained moved north in a single lane. Still there were miles of the city ahead, the whole trip through nothing but what you would call the megalopolis.

"But when you were young," he said. "Before I knew you, when you were young."

"When I was young what?"

"That's when? . . ."

He did not complete that thought, and she did not respond. He had the lights on. They cast a dull glow before the car. A sign appeared, its surface plastered with snow.

"That's the end of the divided," Flora said.

He slowed down, and they passed a semi pulled off on the shoulder, leaning to one side.

"This is where you see the lake," she said.

He looked, and there was nothing. Earth and sky, and now the water, too, had merged into one grey. . . . He saw the plow ahead, and quickly they were around it, and the snow was heaped up to the edge of the pavement.

"Should you have passed?" she said.

"Do you want me to follow it all the way? We're not even out of town. . . . Why don't you answer?"

"Answer what?"

"For Christsake!" he said. "For Christsake! What I said before!"

"Did we make love? Well, yes, we did."

"You made love with him!"

"Yes."

"But when? How many times? You said—"

"I said I didn't love him. I said it didn't matter."

"But before . . . before you and I—"

"I said he was just like me. It's true. I didn't trust men, and he didn't trust women. It's easy then."

"Why didn't you trust men?"

"Because I didn't trust you. It was like you'd woken up to the facts of life, and you blamed them all on me."

"That was when we just got married," he said in astonishment.

"You were so passive then, so easily frightened."

"We were just married."

"And you blamed me—as if it were my fault the gods didn't smile on your every thought! You felt so sorry for yourself! You didn't make me feel like a human being!"

They drove up a hill, and at its top he saw a clump of trees like a shadow, the ghost of a house. A man leaned on the door to a garage, then turned in what seemed slow motion and with his hand outstretched groped his way towards the house. He moved so slowly against the invisible force of wind, leaning against it, outlined there at the top of the hill, that it seemed as if he could not move at all. Then they were atop the hill, and the wind hit them, and for a moment they seemed to stop, to sheer off towards the shoulder.

Fighting the wheel, he had the impression that the wheel no longer mattered and that the wind was going to sweep him sideways off the bank. A car appeared out of nowhere and sloughed on ahead.

"What the hell!"

He could see no road, nothing. Then it was clear again, and he was on the road, and the man and the house had disappeared behind. . . . No one spoke, as if each were not sure what he had seen. There was another hill, but at its top no house and no raging wind.

"It's slippery," said Flora, clearing her throat. "When the wind blows like that I feel us on our little planet flying through space. And everything—so vast, so dark, so cold."

He tried the brakes, hitting them a little too hard, and the car broke free with a sickening ease and glided down the road. It was an effortless glide, as smooth as silk—they might have been floating on a cloud. Just as easily they sloughed around, and without his having moved the wheel he was back on his own side heading down the road. He had not moved. The car had got back on the tracks all on its own. The speedometer said 25—yet in that moment of breaking free he had felt their terrible speed, his utter helplessness before the perverse whimsy of ice and wind.

He glanced in the mirror, and Flora sang to the drowsing child.

Frère Jacques, Frère Jacques,
Dormez-vous. . . .

Ahead on the road danced a vortex of snow.

Dormez-vous,
Dormez-vous. . . .

The car passed through it and then through another.

Sonnez la matine,
Sonnez la matine. . . .

Still a third danced before them—when a car out of nowhere hurtled on down the road ahead.

Din dan don,
Din dan—

He had stopped! Yes, he was sure of it, the car had stopped!

"Alex," said Flora. "Alex, we're in a snowbank."

"What happened, Daddy? Where are we?"

He sat there dumfounded. The headlights were out, and he could see nothing. There had been no impact. They had just stopped. Jeanie began to cry.

"Alex, what? Alex, where?—"

He opened the door, and as it tore out of his hands, he grabbed at it, and it yanked him out of the car. Then as if it had a will of its own, it slammed shut. What had happened? The wind came from all sides, and he crouched in it, grasping his coat, looking around, unable to see. What was he to do? Hurriedly, with thick fingers, he buttoned up, then opened the door and grabbed his hat and gloves.

"Who—"

The door slammed shut. He could hardly open his eyes. He

stood in snow to his knees. He felt at it with his hands like a blind man. Yes, the snow was there. It was solid, yet scarcely distinguishable from the solidity of air. One hand on the car, he moved forward—and found himself floundering to the waist. He had indeed run into a snowbank, part way into a ditch. The wind roared at him. He turned his back on it, bending over and blinking till he thought he could see. The wind was around in front of him again. He thought of that man groping with the blind force of it. He had heard of men in blizzards getting lost between the house and the barn and wandering off till they froze. He felt for the car, patted it to convince himself it was there, then opened the door—his wife and daughter recoiled.

"Oh, Alex."

"Give me the flashlight!" he shouted. "Start the car!"

"Close the door, Alex. Oh, the snow."

She handed him the light as the wind tore the door out of his hand, this time, at her bidding, slamming it shut. He looked about for this person who would torment him with cold and blinding snow in his moment of need. Just when his life was going well. Just when he realized it was all a lie.

He fumbled with the switch. The light glowed faintly, illuminating a small area like a halo. He poked it this way and that, but could not distinguish the drift from the snow-ladened air. He swore, struck the light against the side of the car, and lost it. The car in response started up. He pawed the ground for the light. The wind tore up the back of his coat, and abruptly he stood up.

He looked about as if he would find this someone who would thrust a cold hand up the back of his coat. He felt offended, abused and mistreated. If he could just see, he thought, hoping to strike a bargain. If he could just find the road. He felt his way backwards, shielding his face with one arm. The snow seemed shallow there. He brushed off a taillight. On his hands and knees he touched something, guessed it was the flashlight, but could not find it. The earth seemed solid. He stripped off his glove, but his fingers were stiff and numb. He stood up, feeling the car and looking about, squinting against the terrible wind. He didn't know where to begin, or what to do. If he could just know where to begin, he thought. He would get them out of this. He would learn to live with the truth.

He looked about for this someone to tell him what to do. A nimbus of light appeared before him like an apparition. He put up his hands, and it hurtled past, out of all proportion, whirling him around as it brushed against his upraised hands with the lightness of a feather. Then it was gone.

There was no sight, no sound of its departure in the general uproar. Yet it had drawn all the breath out of his chest, all the stiffness out of his knees. The wind vanished momentarily, then came back like a wild beast, and gasping for air, Alex stumbled back and sat down abruptly—on the road. He was sitting on the road. And there was the single red taillight of the car, glowing as if it were miles away.

They had turned on the interior lights, and he saw them through the window, their faces rosy.

"What's going on out there," said Flora, when he opened the door.

"Put it in reverse!" he shouted.

She did, and with him heaving at the door, the wheels spun.

"Alex, the cold—"

"Flora, goddamn it, we're stuck in a snowdrift!"

He slammed the door and went down on his knees beside the car and scooped at the snow underneath the back axle, flinging it behind him at the wind till he panted and his arms ached and it hurt to breathe. He did not know how long he had till another semi came up the road a little wide of that last. And the plow—would they see it? Would it see them?

He had to work. He hadn't time to think. He dug again till he panted and sweated, and his arms trembled. His throat ached. He saw them again in the window, his wife's eyes, the hood of his daughter's jacket. Then he saw Jeanie's face pressed to the glass looking out. She was two feet away, and he knew by the great staring eyes that she did not see. She stared straight at him, yet seemed far away, in another world.

He felt inclined to rage at his wife's indifference to his present circumstance. His hands were numb, and he could not feel his fingers. He contemplated this numbness, then fell to digging. He sat back on his heels like a man in church and caught his breath. The wind snatched at it as if it would reach right down his throat. Again he saw them through the frosty window, and he flailed at the snow, hurling it behind him to the wind.

It howled at him. It roared. It shrieked as in pain. He saw it as preeminently human and wondered what he could do to make it happy. He knew that it was not human and that there was nothing.

In every syllable of the wind he heard the plow charging up behind him. He crawled around to the other side of the car and found the snow had drifted in again. The wind cuffed at him, and tore off his hat. He caught it and hammered on the door.

He saw her turn from the child as if he were interrupting some droll tale.

"Back up," he said, his voice faint and unreal, like the voice of someone he had overheard making a perfectly reasonable request of his wife, under the most ordinary circumstances.

They looked at him as if he were a ghost.

"Please, back up," he said.

She put the car in reverse, and the wheels spun on the icy road.

"I'll help push," she said.

"I want to drive," cried Jean, clambering over the seat.

He slammed the door, once his wife had got out, and she caught at his arm, as if but for that she would blow away. She had her hood up and her scarf around her face, and she looked like a mummy.

"Don't let go," he called, holding her against the car.

She made no response. The engine roared, and he heaved at the door. Jeanie pushed on the accelerator, and the engine roared, the wheels spun with a low dull sound. He heaved again, his face buried against Flora's coat. He sensed how frail was her grip, how little she pushed.

"Other side," he called.

She appeared stupified by the storm. Again the engine roared, and the wheels spun dully. He took Flora's arm and groped his way around the back of the car. Then he saw it again, a nimbus of light. She stood there, head-bowed. He held her with both hands, himself rigid before the apparition, about to push her aside at the same time he hurled himself against it in puny and futile sacrifice.

It was a car this time, creeping along five feet away, and he saw the driver's face in the brown light of the dash. The driver appeared not to see them, and Flora was just as oblivious of him and his car. It passed, and the red lights became pinpricks and disappeared in the windy dark.

Still the engine roared. Then without speaking Flora clambered on to the trunk, and as Alex leaped aside, the car backed out of the snowdrift, as if there were no drift there at all.

"What the hell you doing parked in the middle of the road!"

Alex found himself in a blaze of light. The roar of the wind had become the roar of the snowplow. The driver had jumped down beside him and shouted in his ear. . . .

With Flora driving they joined the caravan of cars and trucks and followed the plow down the road. For a long time he could not free himself from the impression he had got when in the sound of the wind he had discovered the sound of the plow, the impression and intimate knowledge that if he stepped to the left and a little behind he would find the bags of paper flakes which eager hands flung up before the fan, and they would turn up the houselights, strip off their costumes, and laugh. He could not escape his impression that all along she knew the secret that would make it all all right. It was a simple thing, as simple as her climbing on the trunk of the car, as simple as his impulse for self-sacrifice.

And he could not think why they had gone to Chicago in the first place, except for her notion, to look at Greek pots.

Women

MOST people born into this life expect to stay out of jail as a matter of course, as if in the book of nature or of destiny it were decreed that they remain free and prosperous men, and Zak Andreas was not one of them. He expected, on the contrary, the law to find him out, and hoped only to put off the moment a day, a week, an hour.

Perhaps as middle child in a family of seven he had grown up unnoticed, without parental guidance, or perhaps his ugly face and cheerful smile had made his teachers at school ignore him as a dunce, but Zak grew up knowing what most men learn to forget, that the judge becomes a justice by the size of his contribution to the mayor's campaign, that the teacher and the doctor and the lawyer and the priest succeed in their professions by their skill in flattery, and that the banker becomes a pillar in the community by foreclosing on his neighbor's house. . . .

Alas, if the world is upside down, what can you call a good man but Scapegrace? So said Boethius in ancient times, and anyone who tells you differently—call the police!

Still, jail was not the place Zak wished to be, any more than he wished to be like other men, finding in each condition a drudgery and a servitude loathsome to his nature. It wasn't his virtue so much as an instinct, which told him that anything as pleasant and easy as this life couldn't be free. People in trouble naturally sought him out, marveling at his liberality, rejoicing in his sympathy, and finding in his unconventional manner a justification for themselves to play at fast and loose, never suspecting that Zak Andreas was in his own way an honest man.

His office on Chicago's south side was at the top of a warehouse, the rest of which accommodated the appurtenances of his construction company, and up the stairs and through the door came all manner of humanity, accountants looking to be paid, lawyers seeking to collect, sheriffs delivering summonses, friends with odd tales—all in the hope of reward. In the outer office a secretary, a poor soul with a nervous affliction, rode herd upon this gang, to say nothing of Zak's unruly accounts. Her nervous condition had manifest itself on the first day of her employment when she realized that the overdraft in parenthesis at the bottom of the last page in the ledger, written in red blood, exceeded her life's wages by a factor of ten. When she saw this she burst out in uproarious laughter, and nothing she has seen since, not the sheriff at the door nor the paddy wagon below in the street, has made her cease in this giddy and unseemly delight. . . .

"Look, why do you come to me?" Zak said to the man who had just sat down in front of his desk. On the telephone three lines blinked silently. "Who's on the second?" he said into the intercom to the secretary in the next room. "Tell him I've got someone here. . . . Tell him he'll have to wait."

The sound of laughter came from the other side of the door, but the man across the desk didn't think it funny.

"Two guys tell you they're going to break your legs, you don't sit still!" he said.

"If you want my advice," said Zak, "call the police."

"That's no good."

"What do you mean, it's no good, it's what I'd do! There's something you're not telling me."

"It's like I said, I'm showing this house, and these guys get out of the car and ask me if I'm the owner."

"What did they look like?"

"Greek."

"What does that mean!" Zak said.

"Okay," said Steve. "Forty years old, black hair, suntanned, heavy-set—Greek, am I right? One guy's wearing a trenchcoat, and the other's got on this T-shirt. I told them I'm waiting to meet a client, and they said they wanted three per cent, half my commission, or they'd break my legs."

"You should have walked over to their car, written down the license, and taken it to the police. That's what you should have done," said Zak.

Steve looked at him. "The hell you say," he said.

"I know what you want," said Zak, "but you don't know what you're asking. . . . Some guy called me once in the middle of the night and told me I was dead. I forgot about it until it happened again, and I called the FBI."

"It scares you," Steve said.

"Of course. I even let them tap my phone. It's funny, because I get a lot of weird calls. Some people I had to tell, but some I let go on and on. You should have heard this one broad. Those guys must have gone nuts. Then one time my car made a funny sound starting up, and I dove out of there in this parking lot with a new suit on. . . . It didn't come with a law degree or a broker's license, did it, pal?"

"My wife, if I told her, she'd die."

"Don't bet on it," Zak said, his face broadening into a grin. "My wife when she heard paid up my insurance. What can I say?" he said then. The three lines on his console blinked. "I think they were freelancing—that's my guess. I think they were trying to get lucky. If you're worried about it, get out of town."

"I come to you as a friend—"

"You come to me—don't give me this!"

"Talk to him, Zak."

"Who?"

"Uncle Teddy."

As if to keep himself from responding, Zak punched one of the blinking buttons and waved Steve away.

"Yeah," he said into the receiver. "Oh, it's you, Ed—no, she didn't tell me." He cupped his hand over the receiver and waved Steve away, but Steve didn't budge. "Well, I've got a call in for him now," Zak said. "He's made the commitment, but he's waiting on the CDs from New York . . . Certified

Deposits—I don't know. Soon as I hear, I'll cut the check, okay? . . . In a day or so, I'll call you. . . ."

There was commotion in the outer office, and before he'd punched another line, a man burst through the door. He was fiftyish, in work clothes, and he had only one eye.

"I want my money," he said, coming to the desk. "You expect me to wait in line—I got work to do, and you promised me two months ago—"

"Johnny, you don't listen," Zak said. "I told you I'd pay you as soon as I settled with the bank."

"That was last month!"

"Well, he just got back from vacation," Zak said. "I'll get you the money in a day or so, only do me a favor, huh? Don't let your wife call down there anymore. They don't know what she's talking about, the food, the kids, the lawnmower."

"They won't let her pick up that lawnmower unless she pays cash!" Johnny said. "It's in at the shop."

"Johnny," Zak said.

"I know, I know," said Johnny.

"Go see Jablonski at the Marriot, he had a little fire."

"That's what I need, a nice fire job."

"I'll see you, pal. . . ."

On the console three lines blinked.

"Women," Zak said to Steve. "This guy's a contractor, and I owe him five, maybe eight grand. So his wife calls down to the bank and tells the Vice President how she needs money to buy food, to pick up the lawnmower to cut the grass. It's the kind of call I get a hundred times a day, but this guy at the bank—he can't take it, right? So he decides he needs two weeks out west. He's the only one who can approve my draw to pay this idiot, and because of the lawnmower call he's got to go to Palm Springs for a month. Women!"

The secretary buzzed to tell him the tailor had arrived, and already his mother and sister were coming through the door from the lobby where they had been waiting, for he had promised them each a new dress. Then the tailor was saying that he thought he had come to be paid on an old bill, and Zak was explaining how he'd settle the whole thing in a few days. Just give him a week, he said, but in the meantime he wanted something for his mother.

His sister was a black-haired, white-skinned girl, who adored her little brother for arranging this private fitting far more than if he had sent her to the best dress shop in town, and while he teased her and coaxed her, and cajoled the tailor, Steve buttonholed his mother.

"Is a nice man," Zak's mother said, smiling sweetly, when Zak returned. "Me like your friend too much, Zakarias. Me think you call Little Theodore."

"Ma," said Zak, steering her in the direction of her daughter.

"He looks like a pig," his mother said in Greek. "One can see in his face he has a wicked heart. Tell your uncle to break his legs."

The secretary stood in the doorway and chuckled.

"Your wife's on the phone," she said.

"What's so funny?" said Zak, and picked up the receiver. "I know I said I'd call," he said, "but my telephone was unplugged, and I overslept. . . . Then we can go out of town, if you don't want your mother to know. . . . We could fly out west. . . . Because I feel like a Marguerita, that's all. . . ."

The secretary came in with some checks for him to sign, and he did so without looking. Across the room the tailor displayed a bolt of cloth, and Zak's sister squealed with delight.

"That was my sister," Zak said into the receiver, "you think I entertain women in my office? . . . What would I do with them here?" he exclaimed in exasperation. "Did you ever think about making love in an airport? Well, think about it sometime, because that's what it would be like. Besides, Dorie would only laugh. . . . I think you're getting a little kinky, that's all, Dorie's my secretary. . . . Look—"

He looked at the receiver and hung up.

"Women," he said to Steve. "Why are women always hanging up on me? What are you doing here?"

"Your mother wants you to call your uncle," Steve said.

"Who said he was my uncle?"

"Everybody knows that!"

"Sure. You know, too," said Zak, "and now you're telling me. . . . You know who told you that? Some guy in a barbershop reading comic books."

"Call Theodore," Zak's mother said in Greek, across the room.

"You want to know the truth?" Zak said. "My father and his grandfather came from the same island. The place had a hundred people living there—how do I know if we're related or not, I've hardly met the man, but that's not the point. People like you reading comic books—"

"Theodore is not a man to eat dinner with a priest," the old woman murmured.

"If you want to leave town," Zak said, "I could lend you my place in Acapulco."

"You've got a place in Acapulco!" Steve said, and it was hard to tell if it made him happy or mad.

"But if my wife comes down," said Zak, "you've got to stay in the cabana."

"You've got a pool? Can I play golf?"

"Listen to this guy," Zak said. "One minute he's afraid he's going to die, and the next he wants my card to the Bath and Racquet Club."

He punched a blinking line.

"Hello," he said. "You're with the FBI?" He looked at the telephone in disbelief. "Yes, I had in my employ a man by the name of Fitts. . . . His name was Dudley, not Marvin. . . . He never called himself Lorin. . . . He never called himself Lemuel, either, what did he do? . . . He and his girl friend went into a bank in Las Vegas and stole five-thousand dollars!" Zak exclaimed for Steve's benefit. "No, I don't think it's funny, officer, but the last time I was there the same thing happened to me, only in reverse. . . . Well, he hasn't worked for me in about a year, that's all. . . . No. . . . No. . . . Good-bye."

Steve looked at him.

"He was one of these kids from Africa," Zak said, when he'd hung up. "He speaks English better than you and me together, so I hired him to park cars in a lot I had a piece of, and the people howled because he was black. I told him to keep his nose clean, and one night he was dropping some keys at this psychiatrist's office next door, and there's the psychiatrist bumping his patient on the couch. The next day the shrink screamed, threatened to jump his lease if we didn't fire the kid. I told my partners what had happened. 'Look,' I said, 'this is the way it is,' but I had only five per cent of that deal then, and the shrink had twelve cars at a hundred bucks a month."

"What can you do!" Steve said, and shrugged.

"I'll tell you what I did," said Zak, leaning across his desk. "I told Dudley I'd take care of it, but he got mad and sued the shrink, and the lawyers laughed in his face. That was before First National put up its tower, and we were right next door. I had only a little piece then, but I heard how First was looking, so I went and bought the thing from those partners and sold it to First for a quarter more."

"A quarter of a million?"

"Those guys were so happy to get out of it, and when they realized what I did, they died. They thought I'd stabbed them in the back, the greedy bastards—they'd forgotten all about this kid. When they catch him in Vegas, he's going to call me, I guarantee you, and you know what? I don't care where he is, California or Mexico, I'll get him a lawyer. I owe him something. If those guys hadn't fired him, I never would have figured out what idiots they were, or made that quarter."

Steve made a face.

"It's true," said Zak. "I think it's funny, that's all, him trying to get lucky in Vegas. But seriously, if you want to get out of town—"

"I'm serious," Steve said. "Two guys threaten me, I'm a very serious man."

"I could get you a suite at the MGM. Booze in the bar, mirrors on the ceiling. . . . In a place like that, even you could get laid."

"Who wants to get laid when you're scared to death?" Steve said.

"Takes your mind off your problems. Have you ever been out there?"

Steve met his eye and looked away.

"What, did you get wiped out?" Zak said. "I bet it was a woman—it's written all over your face, pal. So figure, how much did it cost—five, ten thousand? Remember that quarter we were talking about? In three years I'll have paid that to my wife. What's the matter?"

"My wife found out," Steve said, "and she wants a divorce."

"That was an expensive weekend," Zak said.

"Why do you sit here talking like a priest?" his mother said in Greek. "Why don't you throw Good-for-Nothing out and go make money?"

"Ma," Zak said.

"What did she say?" said Steve.

"Ma, it's not polite to talk Greek. . . . My mother," Zak said to Steve, by way of apology. "She thinks to make money I've got to go carry bricks."

"Why do you pass time in the office with a beast?" she said. "In office you spend money. Like your father, God bless his soul, you make money on a job."

Zak punched the intercom.

"Call my broker," he said to the secretary.

But in order to get a free line, he had to talk on the phone.

"No, I can't come to dinner tonight, Godmother, I'm busy," he said. . . . "I'd love to come tomorrow, too, but I'm tied up. . . . It's my godmother," he whispered to Steve. "She makes *souvlakia* you wouldn't believe—no, Godmother, I just can't, I've got to go to New York, my son's got football practice, and my wife's lawyer wants me to come to his office. . . . No, her lawyer, he's an old friend of mine, we went to high school together, and he wants us to get married again. . . . No, the next weekend, let me see—we'll probably be getting married that weekend, Godmother. . . . I think so, Godmother. . . . I'll invite you to the wedding.

"She wants me to marry her niece," he said, as he dialed on the open line. "The girl's gorgeous, she makes thirty grand a year, and she's a virgin at twenty-five."

"So why not?" said Steve.

"Who ever heard of a gorgeous, twenty-five-year-old virgin? She must be nuts—hello, James? Zak. What have you got for me? . . . What about MacDermot? . . . What about TransOceanic? . . . What about MalCo? . . . Look, all I want is a couple of g's to pay my tailor, can you swing it? . . . Talk to you tomorrow, pal.

"I want to show my mother I can make good dough sitting on my tail, and I drop fifteen big ones. I ought to go back to humping bricks."

"Zak, I'm begging you."

"You come to me because you're scared to be seen on the streets, but you won't listen to my advice. You're afraid what people will think, but you think I can go and knock on someone's door, and there's no problem there."

"You know those guys, Zak."

"The guys in the car?"

"You know what I mean."

"The man is a beast," his mother said in Greek.

"Ma," said Zak.

"If the man is a snake, you must carry a stick."

"Ma, please."

"What did she say?" said Steve. "Call him, Zak. She's on my side."

"If the snake crosses the road, drive the cart over his back."

"At least that way you can find out," Steve said.

Zak looked at him.

"Find out what?" he said. "There's something you're not telling me. There's a reason for all this, and you want me to stick out my neck."

"Zak, I swear to God—"

"You owe these guys, and you don't want to pay. You're fishing for something—is it the Vegas thing?"

"Zak—"

"You guys amaze me," Zak said. "How do you get that way?"

"If you have to dig a grave," his mother said, "hire a gravedigger."

"If a guy owed you money, you'd expect him to pay," Zak said. "You'd hire a lawyer, take him to court. So these guys come to collect, and you scream like a girl. They make you a gentlemanly offer, and you don't have the grace to know you're being treated like a human being. If you don't give them three percent, I think they ought to break your legs."

Steve looked at him, and Zak looked away.

"The snake would be a bird," his mother said, "if he weren't a snake."

"Ma," said Zak.

"What did she say?" Steve said.

"Never mind what she said—"

"If the snake would be a bird, he would still eat eggs."

"Ma, for christsake!"

"I like your mother," Steve said. "We understand each other."

He looked at her, and she smiled sweetly. Zak punched the intercom.

"I've got to get out of here," he said to the secretary, "they're driving me nuts. . . . Hey, Connie," he called to the tailor, "can you hurry it up? Don't put me on the elevator now, I know how we stand."

He pulled a bill out of his pocket and handed it to his sister, told her to take her mother to lunch. There was a flurry of thank-yous and kisses good-bye, and when they were gone, Steve remained. . . . The sound of laughter came through the door.

"Ralph's here," the secretary said over the intercom.

"How long has he been waiting?" Zak said. "Tell him . . . never mind, I'll be out in a minute. . . . You've got to go," he said to Steve. "Look, it's simple. You tell him, next time you see him, 'Okay, you'll get your three percent.' It's only money, pal. It's better than being dead."

"I can't," Steve said.

Zak looked at him.

"What do you mean you can't? You sold the place, took your commission, and didn't pay? I don't believe it!"

"I needed the money," Steve said.

"I don't believe what you're asking me!"

"Zak, I swear to God, if my wife finds out. . . ."

"You want me to pay him."

"Just a loan."

"You're worried about your wife, but I don't have a care in the world, I suppose. How much?"

"Five. I'll pay you back in thirty days, with interest."

"Oh, sure, with interest," Zak said, and punched the intercom. "These guys are going to break your legs, but you're afraid of your wife. She must be something. . . . Make one out of First for five," he said into the intercom, "and bring it in to me. . . . Look, are you going to argue with me, too?" he said into the receiver. "I know he's here. . . . I know why he's come. . . . Look—"

He looked at the telephone, and laughter came from it.

"Women," said Zak, glaring at her as she came in with the checkbook. "Why are women always laughing at me?"

She lay the checkbook down in front of him and stood back, laughing to herself.

"What's this supposed to mean?" he said. "I said five, not five dollars. Five is five—five big ones. Whoever heard of five dollars!"

She pointed to the figure in parenthesis below the last entry, and chuckled.

"Will you let me handle that?" he said, and voided the check and wrote out another. "Women," he said under his breath.

Steve watched as Zak wrote out the figure, forming his zeroes slowly and clumsily, until the number looked as if it had been written by a child. Zak signed his name and tore the check out of the book.

"Is he waiting out there for you or me, pal?" he said.

Then Steve was gone, and Zak sat alone in his office waiting for the intercom to buzz. The secretary opened the door and stood looking at him with a quizzical little smile.

"Ralph's here," she said.

"Hold my calls," said Zak.

She stepped aside, and through the door came a young man in a shiny leather coat, with bright blue eyes.

"Nice company you keep," he said, nodding over his shoulder, where they could still hear Steve making his way down the stairs.

Zak waved it away. "Didn't Johnny tell you?" he said.

"They tell me different," said Ralph.

"What can I say," Zak said. "I'm not saying you, Ralph, but once in a while people ought to listen."

"I don't know, Zak. I got to go by what they say. . . ."

They sat in silence.

"You know, in a week or ten days," Zak said, "I'll get this thing settled at the bank, and I'm taking off. They've got the examiners sitting on them, and they can't make a move, but once this thing goes. . . ."

"Sure, take a run out west," Ralph said.

"I'm going to lie in the sun, play a little golf. Forget about the dogs, the tables—forget about everything. I'm serious, Ralph, I'm not going to gamble. Maybe I'll see a show."

"No problem. We'll set it up."

"Maybe I'll run down to the Bahamas, go fishing all day."

"I'll work on it this afternoon," Ralph said.

"Say in two weeks," said Zak. "I'll get this thing at the bank, and, Ralphie, I'm in the peach orchard."

"I'll put the whole thing together, and you can stay as long as you want. . . ."

They sat in silence. Neither spoke.

"I think if you made it out this week in five checks," Ralph said then, "that way if there's a minor problem like last time, it won't become too major."

"Minor problems," Zak said, pawing through the clutter of his desk. "That guy who was in here—you should've heard him. He's scared his wife's going to cut him up in little pieces."

"She already has," Ralph said, "and he don't know it."

"He's a very successful man, you know. His brother's the head of a bank. But he reads comic books, goes to the movies, and he thinks that explains a whole lot."

"Some guys make a living out of tears," Ralph said.

"Then he comes in here and expects me to solve his problem."

Ralphie permitted himself an indulgent smile.

"I can't even solve my own problems!" Zak said.

"Not without the fresh. Not without the green stuff. Is he a friend of yours?"

"Of course he's a friend of mine," Zak said.

"Let me tell you a sad little story about your friend," said Ralph. "He goes out west, stakes his limit, and loses. So I go to him and say, 'Let's set up a program to take care of it.' Then the guy don't pay. He stays out of touch. So who's the villain in this piece of comedy! They're ready to listen, but he's got to have a program, and, hey, he's got to do it! That's what they like about you, Zak. Sometimes there's a minor problem, but things don't get out of hand. Now he tells me he'll see me in an hour, he's got to go to the bank. If you ask me, he ought to find himself a hospital."

Without seeming to listen, Zak wrote out the checks and passed them across the desk, while Ralph pulled out of his coat a leather bank purse and stuffed the checks inside. He rose to go.

"See you next week," he said, and went out the door.

Zak swung in his chair and stared out the window at a cloudless sky.

"Are you here?" the secretary said, chuckling faintly from the doorway.

Zak didn't answer, and she came to the desk, picked up the checkbook, and chuckled.

"You didn't fill in the amounts," she said.

He looked at her sardonically.

"What's so funny?" he said.

"Nothing," she said, unable to restrain her laughter.

"You think I'm nuts, don't you?"

"No," she said, and each word made her laugh a little more.

He smiled and shook his head.

"Why should I fill in the amounts?" he said, looking at her

with a mixture of irritation and amusement. "It's ridiculous already. It's out of the picture. If I fill in the amounts, I might as well jump out the window!"

By now she was laughing so hard she could hardly speak.

"You think I'm crazy," he said.

"No," she said, wiping away the tears. But when she looked at him, she laughed some more. "What are they going to do?" she said in a small voice.

He looked at her with complete disgust.

"Do you think those guys are stupid?" he said. "They're not like these banks; they know I'm good for it. Besides, Ralphie's a friend of mine. Don't be an idiot like Steve. I'm going to have a drink—want to come?"

He looked at her with a kind of curiosity, as if he had never really seen her before, but when he saw the open, vulnerable look on her face, he looked away.

"If you filled in the amounts," she said, walking a fine line of limited sobriety, "maybe I could lend you the money."

"Women," he said, and stood up to go. "Could you lend me two-hundred-sixty-five grand? Could you lend me even eighty grand? So let's not talk about it. I'm getting out of here—want to come?"

"I could lend you five," she said.

"You've got five-thousand dollars?" he said, and sat back down. "You'd lend it to me? How much do I pay you, for christsake!"

He looked at her, but not at her so much as through her, while he made some obscure calculation in his head.

"What about your husband?" he said.

"He doesn't have to know. I mean, you could pay me back sometime, I suppose, couldn't you?"

He didn't answer, but by the look on his face he was again making obscure calculations.

"How soon can you get it?" he said. "Shoot it into my personal—no, into Incorporated. That way Ralphie won't get it, and with five down we'll buy a train load of soybeans and turn it over in a week, and you'll triple your dough. What about that drink? No, you've got to run to the bank. Can you get it there by three?"

"When will you be back?" she said, when he had begun again to move.

"Monday."

"Today's Wednesday!" she said, and all sobriety departed.

"Maybe Tuesday," he said. "I'll catch the late flight. Did you make the reservations? Two, tonight, to Acapulco. My wife," he added, with a funny look. "I'll call you. . . ."

It was a little like curing your nervous affliction by setting your house on fire. So she made the deposit, and when she figured the new balance, it hadn't made a dent, and there were two more checks out of the book where he hadn't filled in the amount. . . .

So Zak went to Acapulco with his ex-wife, and maybe he'd get lucky at the track, and maybe Steve's check would slide through, and maybe Johnny would get a downstroke on some nice fire job so that his wife could pick up the lawnmower. Maybe the whole world would just keep on turning, and for another few hours they'd all stay out of jail, or hospital, or the nut house, but what made it turn? And upon what did their chances rest?

"What's so funny?" her husband said that evening after dinner, looking up from his paper to where she, in the middle of the room, for no particular reason, had begun to giggle.

The funny thing was, she couldn't even tell him. . . .

Women! She'd probably call it kindness. Or Truth or Beauty with a capital letter. . . . Instead of talking to them, just call the police!

Squid Soup

LILY Bogost began to see a lot of her husband after their divorce. She kept the house on East Bay Lane, and Johnny took an apartment downtown, but still he called in the morning, brought her fish from the market, or fresh rolls and bread, and took her out to dinner every week. She told him, in fact, that if she had divorced him ten years earlier, their marriage might have worked, and when he said that it could work still if she'd give it half a chance, she shook her head and said she didn't love him any more, could never love anybody, because she had lost her illusions about men.

As for love, if her sister had a dinner party and an odd man, Johnny babysat with the kids, and Lily came home to find him asleep on the couch. Maybe she'd sit down beside him while he put on his shoes, or maybe she'd make him a cup of tea for the drive home, but one thing led to another so that he stayed the night. Her sister had dinner parties and odd men because she wanted Lily to remarry, and the result was that Lily and Johnny ended up in bed together more often than ever, and more passionately, too, because for him there was the suspicion of whom she had just been with, and for her—well, since she had no more illusions, she had no more restraint.

Restraint had been a problem, too, and not because she didn't like sex. When you got married you declared your choice, and half the fun in life came from not knowing what you were going to do, or where you were going to do it. Then the big surprise was when you said, "No!" and pretty soon that wasn't a surprise anymore, either. Now he was only angry if he came to babysit and the telephone rang with strange men asking where she was.

"Oh, him," she said, when he'd thrown a name in her face. "We went out to dinner, and he didn't like squid. A man who doesn't like squid—all he'd want from me would be oral sex."

Johnny went white, and then he got very red, and the veins stood out in his neck.

"He didn't like squid, Johnny," she said, because she could see he was upset. "So how could I really like him?"

That was the way things began when she came home from her sister's. Lily talked to him, not as a wife to her husband, but as a woman to her friend, her man friend, if you like. It was on a high level, as far as she was concerned, and if it ended up in bed in the most surprising tangle, that was no more than it should be.

During the week, he was a stockbroker downtown, and though he was thirty-five and athletic, the strain of all this babysitting told. They had separated in the first place because he didn't come straight home from work, and sometimes left the house at five or six in the morning, until it dawned on her that he had a life apart. It didn't matter that he only stopped in for breakfast with his mother, or that he had a drink or two on the way home with an old friend; it only went to prove he was not the man she thought he was but someone tied to the past and the image of himself as a child. It didn't matter that she talked with her mother half the morning on the telephone. Women were different from men, and if they talked to their mothers it was because they wanted to know how to bake the bread or stir the soup, not because they wanted to be little girls again. If they talked with their friends about what their husbands said or did the night before, before during or after they had made love, it was to learn the art of it, not to boast or complain like some high school bully.

No, women were older than men, more reliable and honest. They could do, to be sure, great villainy, but only following great provocation. Men were capable of marvelous things, heights of accomplishment, moments of insight, flashes of brilliant truth, but over the long haul their performance was wonderfully thin, and what was marriage but the long haul? Marriage was not what you could be, or might become. It was not a hope or a promise or a dream. It was what you were. It was truth, and men spent their lives denying or ignoring or altering it.

That was the thing that life had taught her at age thirty, that at ages fifteen and twenty-five it had seemed to deny. Life had said then that men were strong and women weak, that men were dependable and women frivolous and false, and she saw now that it was the other way around, and what made her know it for a certainty was that she didn't even hate him. Women understood life and the nature of consequences, that you paid for your sins to the last drop of blood, while men assumed that with a smile and a handshake, with a sheepish look and a little apology, everything was all right. No, women were an older race, capable of the great truth this life had to reveal, in the face of which men kicked and fought, or simply closed their eyes and begged for mercy.

Like the time the Market fell, and in the course of three days he lost a hundred-thousand dollars and never told her, wouldn't even admit it when she asked.

"But is it true?" she said, in the flush of discovering what everyone else, apparently, knew.

He denied it, called it vicious gossip, and all the while he wouldn't meet her eye. He wasn't protecting her from the truth so much as he was protecting himself. He could not admit what on the instant had become clear to her, that he was not what he pretended and she had believed him to be—proof against the world.

"What are you laughing at?" he said.

"Nothing. I don't mean to laugh."

It was just so comically obvious, and she was laughing at her own blindness not to have seen. She didn't hold it against him. She just wanted a divorce.

Perhaps she did hold it against him a little at first—like the time it snowed two feet and the plow came late, and even though he had moved downtown then, she called him to complain, as if for the weather and the vagaries of human conduct he were to blame. There was something in the inconsistency of weather that suggested to her the masculine spirit: one day furious and cold, the next foggy, insipid. It was the same with things like the plowing service upon which you couldn't depend. Still, a little reflection upon the nature of things suggested that to believe so was to lie to herself, and looking at life with a new awareness, she vowed not to lie.

It meant facing things she had always preferred to ignore, and among these was how much she wanted. She wanted to dress well, to be seen and admired—in short, she wanted money. The men her sister found were usually rich, but when they asked Lily out, if Lily didn't like them, she said no, and when they found this so terribly provoking that they declared their passionate love, she laughed in their faces. Then she had to admit she was not a nice person.

The trouble was, the only man she had ever made love with was Johnny. This, too, she held against him, but she vowed not to hold it against him long. But all the men she met, with their BMWs and their silk shirts, with their fast-food franchises and their apartment houses converted to condominiums, were ridiculous, and when she thought what she meant by this, it was that they were all on diets, or ate nothing but steak, and if she insisted they go to a place where she could have fish, they ordered their sole smothered in white sauce. She didn't like men who didn't like fish, because men who didn't like fish didn't like women or sex.

It was one of those intuitions she discussed with her seamstress, who was the only person who understood.

"First he orders a dry martini?" Gena said, on her knees beside the chair upon which Lily stood holding up the skirt. "That is to express the firmness of his intent, for as everyone knows, gin makes things hard and straight which are otherwise irresolute. Tell me what he orders next."

To look at them, you would call them mother and daughter, but in fact Gena was younger, and only her husky voice and grave demeanor made it appear otherwise. Two years before, her husband had died, and following the custom of Greek women, she had worn black ever since.

"Next he ordered those little cheese things on toast," Lily said, "while I had conch in vinegar and oil."

"After a meal and not before is the time for things rotten and decayed," Gena said, her fingers full of pins. "But sea snail expresses a readiness for love."

This Lily didn't understand, until Gena explained it.

"Isn't the snail soft?" she said, "and isn't that why he looks for a house? The walls of the house bristle with defense, but on the inside they are smooth and pink. It is the same with a woman. If he drinks gin, then eats cheese before the meal, he will reach his conclusion before the proper end and be no use to you in bed."

There was a ritual involved, a necessary ordering, with each thing in its place.

"Because after the beginning comes the middle," Gena said. "If a man forgets this, he reaches the end too quickly, and you have to start all over again. But who wants to eat oysters after meat?"

It was funny, because Lily felt closer to Gena then than to her own sister, Leah, who, when she arrived, expressed impatience with the way Gena talked. About her own husband, on the other hand, Leah spoke with irony and contempt.

"Three times he made love to me last night, and I never felt a thing," she said. "Then this morning he wanted to start all over again. . . . Why do you look at me, Lily? I'm as sore as a shoe."

Gena never spoke except to ask, was the hem too low? But when Leah left, it was another matter.

"She wants you to marry," Gena said then, "so that she will

have your husband."

"She doesn't even like Johnny," Lily exclaimed.

"All the same," said Gena.

"She won't speak to him except to argue. If he would come, and she were here, in two minutes they would fight!"

Gena closed her mouth and said no more, but from Lily's point of view she was wonderfully mistaken. Her sister loathed Johnny—hadn't Leah told her so a hundred times, understood her dissatisfaction, encouraged her divorce? What's more, Leah was just like Johnny, outspoken, headstrong, proud. There were never two people so unsuited. No, Gena was comically wrong.

"I didn't say suited," Gena said. "But when you marry, she will take him."

If Leah and Johnny were not suited for one another, Lily and Johnny were, in Gena's opinion, and this Lily found even more impossibly strange. All the years of their marriage they had done nothing but squabble, about what time he would leave in the morning, about when he would come home at night, about whom he was seeing, and how often he lied, until she did not know any longer what to believe.

"Of course he lies," Gena said. "Isn't he a man! Men believe in things. Of course!"

"Leah's husband doesn't lie."

"Because he doesn't love her."

"He makes love three times a night!"

"Does she like it? . . . So, you see? He doesn't know what love is. A man lies."

Leah's husband bought and sold gold, and his conversation was an account of the day's fluctuations, all his moves on the Exchange. As the price had steadily risen for seven years, their friends thought Leo a genius—but not Leah. Still, the week Johnny had lost a hundred-thousand, Leo had made the amount five times over on the Exchange, a fact which Leah threw up at her sister if she suspected her of wavering in her resolve. It wasn't that money was everything, Leah said. But if your husband left early in the morning and stayed out late with the boys, then lost all those dollars in no more time than it takes to lose your hat, what remained? Lily could hardly bring herself to think the word *sex.* Nevertheless, when Leah pressed her, she said it.

"You make love with him?" Leah exclaimed, unable to believe her ears. "Where? When? How many times?"

She acted as though Lily had betrayed all that they had stood for and meant to each other, as sisters, and when Lily told her where, when, and how many times, there were tears in Leah's eyes.

She stopped having dinner parties, and as Lily no longer went "just to my sister's," Johnny no longer babysat. It wasn't that she lost all opportunity to go out; it was just that dating meant intentions and intentions meant that whole slow, fateful progress of relationships, with all those responsibilities, with all those commitments and decisions. She did not want to date, but decided that she had to, just so Johnny would babysit. When he objected to this, she took to calling him late at night on the pretext of the children.

Sometimes he answered, his voice heavy with sleep, and sometimes the phone rang and rang. She couldn't tell which she liked less, his ability to sleep or her own not knowing where he was, and when she thought about it, she ceased to know if the tickle in her daughter's throat was merely an excuse or tuberculosis.

"I must have been asleep," Johnny said, explaining how the phone could have rung and rung. "I got back from dinner, and dozed off with the TV."

"You went out to dinner—with an old friend, I suppose."

"You've met Jack. I saw him downtown, and we stopped for a drink."

"And then you went home to bed?"

"First we had dinner."

"Did you have a drink before or after?"

"Well—both."

"And I suppose you met someone there."

"I've got to eat, don't I?" he said. "If I see someone, am I not supposed to talk!"

"I just want to know why, when your son comes down with

the measles, you're nowhere to be found."

"I thought it was Paula."

"Well, Joey hasn't been well."

A month ago he would have protested her unreasonable demands, but now his silence was full of guilt, and she sat bolt upright in bed and knew. . . .

"Of course. Your sister," Gena said the next day. "You must decide what to do."

There was nothing to decide, Lily said. She would never see them ever again. How could a husband be so perfidious? Just when she was ready to admit that she missed the man. And a sister—but how could she stoop so low!

Leah, when she confronted her, swore it wasn't so, demanded to know who would spread such a lie! Johnny was less indignant. He flushed crimson and said if he had gone to see Leah, it was because he loved Lily.

"I don't even like your sister," he confessed. "She asked me to lunch—said she wanted to talk about you."

Lily looked at him with arched eyebrows, and he would not meet her eye.

"Sometimes I get confused," he stammered. "I mean, if I'm married to you, why am I living downtown, and if we're not married, then when I see a woman—"

"Don't be a prude!" she cried. "We're talking about my sister!"

She felt the top of her skull rise, and when she could see again, there he was before her, a weak, pathetic, nervous, spineless man. Leah persisted in vehement denials, called it Johnny's latest fabrication, and unable to decide whom she hated more, Lily decided to murder them both. Knives were out—she preferred her bare hands. And then she knew that if she had them to dinner she could poison their soup. . . .

Neither guessed that the other was coming, and once they had all arrived, there was Leo with his recital of the day's machinations to paralyse the atmosphere and prevent any bolting.

"First you serve wine," Gena said, who had come to handle the kitchen. "It draws the spirit out of its shell like the head of a turtle. But for yourself, gin for firmness and strength."

Lily had read in the newspaper that murders were committed on gin, and as she drank from the glass Gena handed her, in which floated a wedge of lime, she found her intentions firm and strong. Graciously smiling, she made sure everyone's glass was full.

"Then oysters," Gena said, back in the kitchen. "Something raw and slippery for subtleness and guile." And before Lily left, she made her drink down the smooth, delicate, passionate meat.

Lily placed the tray upon the table and instructed the others to partake. She did not always understand the things Gena said, but when Leo broke off his monologue and said that, oh, ho, ho, he knew what she had in mind! she met his leering look with a subtle smile and understood the usefulness of guile.

"Next comes soup," Gena said, when Lily had them all seated. "Into the soup you put squid cut in little pieces. Last you put the ink."

Lily looked to know if this was the fatal portion, and could tell nothing from Gena's face. At the table all waited for her to begin, and with her spoon raised she stared at the bowl before her, from the surface of which protruded a carrot, a tomatoe, a bush of tentacles. In the liquid of the bowl her discerning eye found black ink.

"It smells like fish," Leo observed, "but it tastes like chicken."

Leah, too, found it to her tooth, and even Johnny seemed glad to have something that wasn't going to explode in his face.

"You're not eating, my dear," Leo said to his sister-in-law. "If you don't eat such a meal as this. . . ."

She looked at them in the glow of candlelight, and did her eyes deceive her, or did they smile? The gin had made her firm, the oysters slippery and devious. Gena appeared in the doorway and nodded her approval. Lily closed her eyes and ate.

There were other things as well, things roasted, things

baked, and when at last they had taken their fruit and ricotta upon the terrace, the night was balmy, and the air seemed liquid as it touched her skin. Overhead, the stars looked wet and close like fireflies amidst the trees. She forgot who was supposed to live and who to die, and in the darkness, in the hushed summer's night her whole self expanded and dissolved, as Johnny whispered breathlessly, hopelessly, in her ear.

"Please," he said. "I didn't know. . . . Forgive me."

On her feet she found she could not walk, and then she did not need to walk. She couldn't say where her sister had gone, but the stone was cool against her cheek, and she did not know how her dress had come undone, but she had never felt the rough-smooth texture of terra cotta on bare skin.

"Please," he said, his hand groping over her arm, her side, her leg, until she steadied it and showed him the place. "From now on I promise. . . . Just one more chance. . . ."

At noon the next day when she came downstairs, she half expected a dining room full of corpses, and she herself felt only partially arisen from the dead.

"Of course," said Gena, in the kitchen washing up. "From raw to cooked to rotten—love commits its own little murder, which is a sweet revenge. With such a meal you have stolen the soul right out of his body."

It had to do with things in their proper place, with admitting what you really wanted. All she had to decide now was whether she should enjoy her revenge and take her husband back, or have a little mercy and never see the man again.

Gena's Squid Soup

3 garlic cloves
1 chopped onion
1 green pepper
1 bay leaf
sautéed in ⅓ cup olive oil

add 3 lbs. squid cut in rings
1 lb. chopped tomatoes
whole shrimp
mussels in shell
clams in shell
whole crab
Red Fish cut in chunks

season with parsley
basil
fennel
saffron
Italian hot peppers

add 1 cup white wine
1 cup water

cover and steam

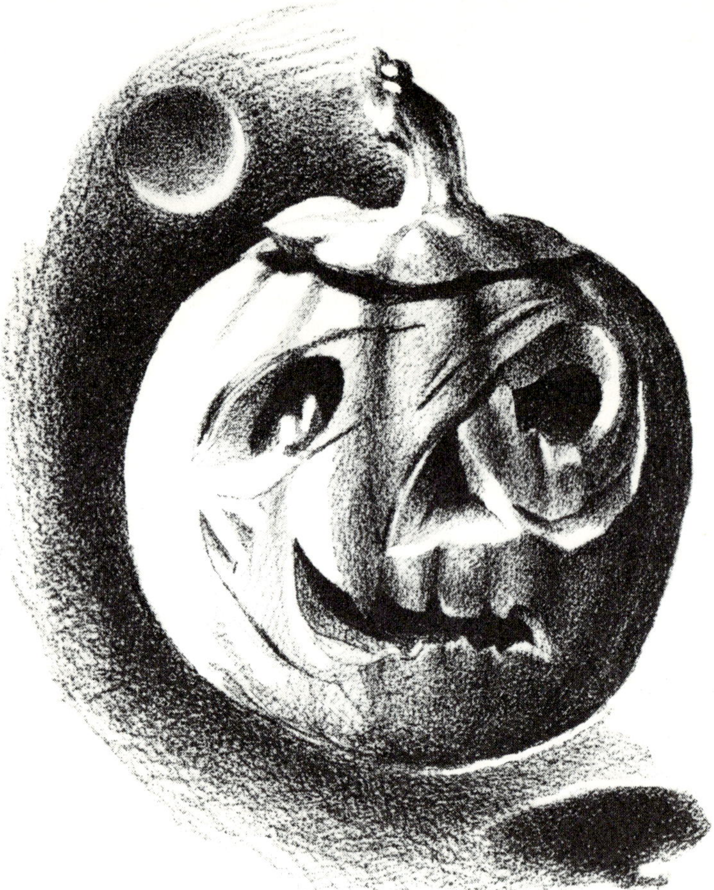

Laughter

EVERY town should have a place like Tony's, that served veal with tomatoes and eggplant, spaghetti marinari, and crabs or clams when they're in season, porgy or slabs of tuna you could eat raw, it made your mouth water so to look at it, and homemade wine. People thought nothing of driving a hundred miles just for dinner, and yet it was a place you would drive by every day and never notice, unless you happened to remark the number of Cadillacs in a warehouse district down by the river.

Even when word spread, not everyone liked his vinegar and oil without any sugar, or his marinari with fresh basil and all that garlic. Still, the attraction was not only the food, which was the best in all the world, but the entertainment.

Tony had a singer named Lila who came on at nine and sang "Good-bye to Yesterday" and "My Man," "Let's Call the Whole Thing Off" and "What a Night, What a Moon, What a Girl"—blues songs. Then around ten-thirty, Lila sat down, and if by eleven nothing else had happened, she sang again till midnight. Usually around eleven there came out from behind the bar a comedian who talked to the patrons as long as the inclination served him, and few ever departed before he was done.

He was not a Las Vegas comedian with jokes and a set kind of patter, and when he spoke to the people around the bar, no one went away feeling that he had been held up before the light for all to gaze upon, not even the biggest crook in the bunch whose M.O. he had spelled out to the letter. I may not have mentioned that this was a tough place, which I attribute to Tony and his brother Rico, who had a lot of funny friends who liked to gamble in the back room, friendly games for a g-note a hand. The other thing that made the place tough was the food, for as everyone knows, tough guys like to eat.

The thing about the comedian was that he made no one laugh, or even smile. How he did it was really his talent and his genius, which I cannot explain except to say that his was not the bitter humor that springs from disillusionment, nor the sweet humor that sets on every act the face of innocence. Rather he spoke to all as to the sufferers of a universal doom, and yet his was not a melancholy humor at the foibles of man, nor contempt for this life, but rather he expressed what you might call an appreciation for the vigorous nature of things, the variety and awesome power of people and circumstances and events.

"You take murder," he would say, looking around the room not at any one but at all, because the spotlight was on him and he could not see. "Now some will say that murder is a terrible crime, but I call it a failure of imagination, which is worse. Because if jail is your wish and the place you desire to be, there is an easier way, under terms more advantageous; and just because some people deserve to die don't mean you have to accommodate them. Still, the plow goes through the field and cuts the worm—it's the nature of the plow to cut, and who would teach it otherwise, just as the worm must learn the best in his nature, which is to forgive."

It was not to everyone's tooth, no more than the marinari was, and there was little of the acquired taste about it, either, if you were not bred to such things. For he spoke to all as to the common criminals of this world, not with condescension but with compassion, and especially for those who knew not what they were, as doctors who thought themselves well, lawyers who thought themselves lawful, and priests who thought themselves good.

"There was a man once whose name was Angelo, who tried

to kill his younger brother," he said, with a gesture to the crowd as if to say, these things happen! "I met him in Hell, and when I asked him why he would do such a thing, he said it was because their father did not value his gift as he valued his brother's. So this younger brother ruled their father's heart with meekness and a pretense of virtue, and Angelo's face turned black with the bitterness in his heart. He would do murder, and yet his father had cast around that brother a circle that would not yield to Angelo's intent. And so I say there is an arbitrary will in this world which strives against our nature, and against which we strive, in order to find ourselves. . . ."

Though he was of middle stature and undetermined age, neither young nor old, and though his face was white and his suit shapeless and black, in the manner of a clown, yet his style was heroic. His audience, too, differed from the majority of people, for by nature they preferred not to idle away their time in front of the TV at home, preferred darkness in a neighborhood and the proximity of the river and the smell of garlic; whose domestic arrangements afforded no tranquility, whose souls were stirred with a restless wandering—in short, thieves, con men, dope dealers, prostitutes, sharks—romantic types altogether. And yet the heroic style accorded itself with them, for they believed ultimately in the soft yielding quality of things—that the thunderstorm of today would grow the peach orchard of tomorrow. Though the world this comedian proposed was governed by unmitigable agents and implacable forces, yet in him the human spirit always prevailed. For he was a comedian not in the modern sense of the word but in the ancient, in that he made a man's soul to wax light, not his mouth to laugh. For laughter, as we all know, betokens the humorlessness of materialism and the despair of a world without meaning.

On the nights he did not come out, Lila sang a second set, "Time on my Hands" and "Ghost of Yesterday," and Rico mingled with the crowd or played cards, while Tony went over his accounts with his bookkeeper in back. These were known as "Quiet Nights," in spite of the noise Rico made at the bar. The nights with the comedian when you could hear a pin drop in the breathless pause between his words, which themselves were soft and "old-sounding" though passionate, these nights were described in the lingo of the factory workers who dropped by after work, as "The Whole Machine."

No one save Tony and I suppose Lila knew the comedian's name, for no one save Tony and perhaps Lila put him together with his off-stage life where he was Tony's bookkeeper. Now, some will call it impossible that a bookkeeper could be a comic, and yet I have known bookkeepers to be very funny fellows—but that is not the point. Truly this bookkeeper was one of a kind, even though by day he struggled with ledgers and checkbooks and reams of unpaid bills, muttered under his breath at the carefree habits of Tony who begged him for his financial advice, who even paid him for it on occasion, only to ignore it and in fact turn it upside down—for a whim, for nothing. And yet it was not this recalcitrant material of accounts receivable and bills-to-be-paid which he transmogrified into cosmic forces and then assailed heroically in his imagination. For truly he loved Tony—I was about to say like a brother, and yet I intend here no irony. The force against which he strove was himself.

Seeing him on the street, you would take him for an employee in some shabby establishment, an educated man perhaps in whom a glimpse of the true face of life had withered all ambition, a man in short who had failed. And indeed he had failed, and had fallen, from a considerable height, for his father had been mayor of this town, a host to bankers and bishops, a confidant to chancellors and philanthropists and chairmen of the board, a man of formidable reputation, whose elder son, my bookkeeper's brother, had become a writer of note, a famous novelist, renowned for the weightiness of his thought, a steadfast prop of morality and tradition in the state. His novels were once described by an ardent reviewer as "chief defenders of the institutions of our day." Indeed, his novels might better have expressed themselves in concrete block about the size and shape of a court house, as opposed to our comedian's art, which was all air and words, possessing no more of this world than a moment which was gone as soon as it arrived, existing somewhere between memory and anticipation.

I mention this only to suggest that when the comedian spoke of two brothers and one whose gifts were favored, he spoke with understanding. For not infrequently this elder brother when he was in town came to Tony's restaurant, knowing that his sibling was here employed as a bookkeeper, and, in the patronizing spirit of an older brother, bringing with him his old mother and father and ordering everything there was to have in anticipation that all would be on the house. For these occasions the comedian would prepare a fiery little text. He wanted to show his best, I think, and offer the flower of his talent to the honored table.

Now, whether it was that they delighted so in their food, or had so much to say to one another around that table, I don't know, but when this comedian delivered his piece, no one of his family paid the slightest attention but sat stonily for a little minute and then began to chatter amongst themselves, quietly at first but with less and less restraint, until their laughter quite overwhelmed the brother's act.

This older brother, it seemed, was a wit, and his mother and father agreed that comedians should be funny and among his other talents their elder son should go on the Johnny Carson Show, as indeed he had, more than once.

Of course, they clapped when everyone else clapped, for they were well-bred, accustomed to the form of pleasing manners, and later on when their son and brother had emerged from behind the bar and, wiping the grease paint and powder from his chin, had joined them at table, they greeted him vigorously, offering him a drink (which was on the house) and clapping him on the back and questioning him with an earnestness that lasted only as long as the question, about his job of bookkeeping, the learned writer exclaiming how he himself had need most especially of accountants and tax specialists and investment counselors whom he must consult daily, now that things were going so well, and all the while he spoke his gold rings and watchband and the little pendants he had about his person gleamed in the darkness.

Never once did he so much as mention the words his brother had spoken on stage, or refer by any sign or gesture to his act, so that I took it they did not know their brother and son to be the comedian, had blocked it from their minds, or failed to add two plus two to connect the halves of his life—how can I explain it? It was the strangest thing in the world to watch that bookkeeper's face as he sat with them, receiving their pats on the back at first with modesty and shyness and then with growing confusion as once again the perverse emptiness in his relations with these people impressed him. Then he would grow silent, and remote, and sullen, and at last furiously angry.

Afterwards, he would not come out of his cubicle for three days but would rummage through Tony's accounts as through a bottomless drawer in which he had lost a tiny precious object he could scarcely bring himself to look for, he despaired so of finding it. Night after night Lila would sing the blues until at last you would hear strange murmurs from that little room, and in there was our comedian with big tears running down his face, as if the refrain of Lila's sad song had overwhelmed him and all his impulse with its truth.

Still, on the fourth night he would emerge, his style more heroic than before. As he became leaner and less weighty with this manner of fasting, so he became more fierce—fire and air he strove for against the melancholy humors of earth and water—so that even Lila, who was black, and who showed no emotion not even when she sang, whose face was a somber mask of passive suffering which fate had hollowed out, carving away the inessential and probing the tough fibrous core as it would discover the true nature of the thing, and its beauty—even Lila listened.

So by day this comedian strove with his ledgers and the formless chaotic nature of Tony's finance, and all might have been well had Tony's establishment not been old and most of the clientele on the cuff. Even though Tony had set it up so that no one should go on the cuff, not even himself, so that every bill had to be paid in green paper or silver coin, even when he wished to buy a friend a drink, still Rico made exceptions for so many close friends (and who in that place wasn't close and friendly?) that sometimes it seemed the only cash in the drawer was the cash Tony had just put in when he bought for those guys at the bar.

In the back room with the cards it was different. Tony couldn't add two deposits and one withdrawal and come up with a positive balance, but he knew the odds charts for stud poker to three decimal places. That friendly little game was business, you see, but because it was business it never got entered into the books. Day by day this bookkeeper, then, had to perform minor miracles in mathematics—striving with numbers in precise order against a sheer weight of bills and receipts, against Tony's impulse of friendship and Rico's to skim off the top—and these things that bookkeeper assailed with fortitude and cunning and belief, just as by night he assaulted with words not just what you might call the inertia of family, but all the things in this world which family stood for and was, in spades—law and tradition and institution and everything else which denied and forbade and ignored and said "no." The longer you listened the surer you were that he plotted some act of revolt that would burst through the bands and fling him beyond their ability to ignore him or define him, that would change them utterly and so, too, himself.

Members of the audience, feeling what he meant, offered him advice or the tools of their trade, to assist in perpetrating the crime which they could not conceive but which stirred their imaginations, so that the darkness beyond the single spotlight was alive with shouts of encouragement, electric with the feeling of possibility.

"Do it in an alley," cried one, conveying thereby the sum of his experience and the extent of his wit, and even though he did not know just what was to be done, still his advice was good.

"Drive a semi through their window."

"Cut 'em up in little pieces and bury 'em in the garden."

This the deathless droll advice of him who liked the special tang that compost gave to his *basilico*. . . .

There were other cries as well, and other encouragement, for each had wisdom to impart, the gleanings of a professional lifetime of thrusting himself against the limits of law and order, and yet this comedian ignored them all. What could they assume but that his plot was more subtle! He had no visible profession as far as they were concerned, not a car or a woman or even a horse that he could run in the Pimlico, bet for or against, cripple or dope or paint blue—the ways you could work it were too numerous to mention—nor did he have any of the other manifestations of substance and power that they acknowledged and recognized, but only the gift of words, and so they assumed he was a genius. They were generous creatures, unlike their law-abiding neighbors in this one respect that they appreciated that which they did not themselves understand or possess. It never occurred to any of them except Tony and perhaps Lila that this comedian's revolt was utterly idiotic in its conception—he intended to invite his brother to Tony's bar and strangle him with his fists.

He did it, too, one dark night of the human spirit, delivering first a diatribe on the banality of greatness and the mediocrity of the famous, so poignant a speech that the novelist of note wept bitter tears, nodding up and down most especially when our comedian came to the part about it being the nature of the plow to cut and of the worm to forgive. Still, what our comedian had not reckoned on was that this brother in his fashionable affluence had been going to the gym, or Club as he called it. At first this brother thought our comedian had taken to massaging his burly shoulders, which was no more than he might have expected, it being the nature of the worm to forgive him his greatness. But when, glancing around, he glimpsed the unbridled hatred in his brother's eye, he shrugged him aside as he would some insect that had lighted on his collar, so that our comedian found himself sprawling on the floor.

Any number of the patrons of that establishment leapt up to finish off the job, for they had perceived at once the flaws in our comedian's garroting technique. Before they could produce the necessary wire or leather cord which had been doused with pig urine to make it supple and strong, this famous novelist overcame his momentary revulsion and helped his brother to his feet, speaking to him perhaps more kindly, with more hearty bravado than before, which prompted our comedian to draw from his coat a dagger and lunge at his brother's throat.

The writer of note dodged and parried adroitly, owing to certain fencing lessons he had taken at the Club but also to the natural good grace that was his birthright and his alone (for each, you can see, conceived himself the plow and the other the worm). The murderous weapon skidded across the floor, while our comedian blundered helplessly after it, fetching unceremoniously up against the door to the women's john and Lila's feet, as she was coming out.

Some of the patrons out of their sense of the sheer ineptitude of it all, and some, revering our comedian for his genius and feeling that what had transpired was merely prologue to a great event, and some out of malicious delight to witness another man's fall—they laughed. At first it was a titter, which grew into a giggle, which turned into a chuckle, and then into a chortle. This became a belly laugh, and that loud guffaws, until it passed all the stages of human merriment, and abruptly our comedian sat up.

Never had he evoked anything so degraded as laughter. His had always been an heroic aspiration, to proclaim and be all that was upstanding in the human capability. He had always stood before this crowd as a witness to that exalted life, had known for a certainty that they saw in his shabby clothes and unkempt hair and white powder and paint the pure manliness of his being, which these rude trappings served to highlight and counterpoint. What he felt now was that these patrons were no longer one with him but separate and apart, and that there was in this life no ideal to aspire to but only a foolish pose. Upon this earth there was no longer any mystery, or magic, or meaning, and he was here upon its face utterly alone. He seized the knife that lay beside him, and the gun and the rope and the poisoned soup that willing hands profferred, and he would have killed himself except that Lila stayed his hand.

"What for?" she said.

"Don't you see!" he cried, invoking the enormous injustice of such a hoax of sympathetic camaraderie, such a fantasy of meaning having been perpetrated, of all people, upon him. Words could not express the emptiness and shame for him who had conceived his life differently.

"You made a mistake," Lila said.

She had never thought herself the crown of creation. She had never thought that anyone understood her melancholy songs or forgave her the number of her years or the color of her skin. Rather, she had imagined a vast space full of people and events, an immense river, a deep, and she had lived a little while upon its shore, had heard it speak in all its voices, and had partaken a little in what it brought past, paid homage to it in her song.

"I made a mistake?" said the comedian.

She nodded.

"About life?" he said. "Then. . . ."

He did not say the word but only gestured towards the murderous weapons.

"Never mind about that," she said. "It come soon enough."

So this comedian remained at Tony's place, but in that evening he had unlocked the chest of human laughter and opened that door that is not so easily closed again. Where before no one ever imagined laughing at anything he said, so now they laughed at everything. It wasn't that he said anything new or different. It was just that now it appeared in a new light, a different light, and they wondered why they had never seen that it was terribly funny.

Tony's place grew popular then, and the food became garbage. He had to hire a second cook, you see, and there aren't two cooks in this world who know to keep the sugar out of marinari. Nobody comes to hear Lila anymore, and she waits on tables in the back, where her demeanor suits the few old friends who still gather for that game at a thousand a hand.

Our comedian ceased to be a bookkeeper, too, ceased to believe in the truth of numbers, and Tony bought a cash register that sorted everything out and didn't struggle or murmur or offer advice but only squeaked a little like a machine. His brother, the famous novelist, comes in at least once a week now, bringing with him his old mother and father who enjoy the show enormously. Comedians should be funny, you see. . . .

Laughter! They ought to make a law against laughter.

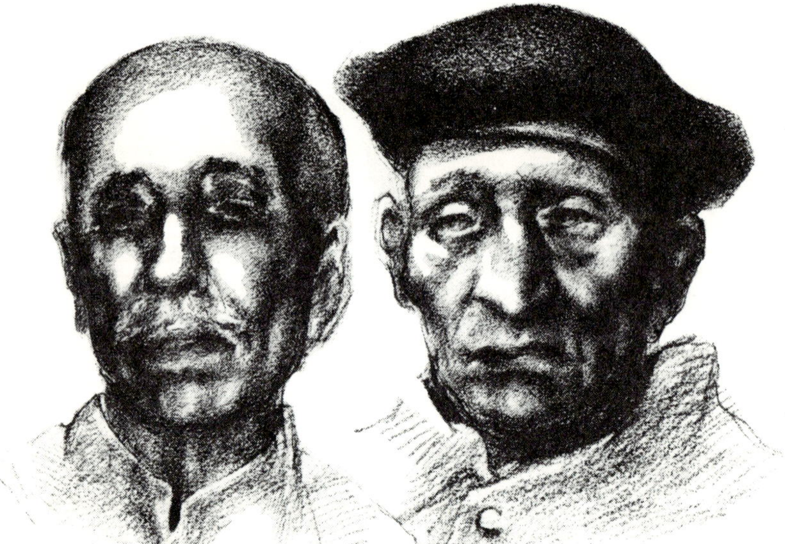

Mr. Georgio, an American

IN the old ward back in the old days Mr. Georgio and Mr. Draghicchio were friends. That was before the city tore the red church down, and we all got rich. None of us wanted them to tear down the church, any more than we wanted to get rich, and when they boarded up her doors we howled and moaned, threw stones at the police, and slept all Sunday morning.

It was the same with the houses in which we lived along those muddy lanes that the city couldn't be bothered to pave, and at night when you went out to the privy you had to mind your manners and say excuse me to the rats. When the city sent in the bulldozers, they had to drag the women from the places before the roof fell down, the way you drag horses from a burning barn, and still they clung to the bedpost and swore they would rather die. So first they bulldozed the church, and everyone made a fuss about saving the Virgin and St. Anthony and resurrecting these things in a new church, God alone knew where.

After the church was down, the city had less trouble with

the women. You would wake up in the morning and discover the house next door empty, or even vanished altogether as if it had never been there, or maybe a tornado had come and left a pile of sticks and not a word of thanks.

At night if you had to go outside, you passed the kitchen and heard your parents whisper, and then one night they bundled you up, and you awoke the next day in a new house in a new bed, and in that house was running water and a toilet that flushed. So you forgot your manners and said excuse me to no one and realized that after all you were rich.

Still, it had to be accomplished after dark, that move, because of the shame of turning your back on your neighbor's poverty. Then when you looked out the window you saw next door your neighbor of before, who had become rich, too. Now, whether that money came because the church no longer took it away, or because your mother found it hiding in the mattress, I don't know, but many swore that, when the church fell down on the priest's head, that money had come from God above in heaven. . . .

Georgio and Draghicchio were friends in the old way, as men are who have no secrets from each other and who discuss matters fully and freely right to the end. In the old ward it was not unusual to hear them on the corner in front of de Palma's market, or on the steps of the church before Mass, and sometimes all through Mass, and Father Stephano would open his throat to sing louder to remind those heathens to listen to the holy words. Still, the best he could hope would be for them to move off down the street, for once they started they never stopped, and one word led to another, and one reason to its opposite, and Georgio would say, "But then there is to consider . . ." for Georgio was a reasonable man, very grave and a little simple if the truth be told, and so Draghicchio would counter, "And yet I heard Luca say . . ." which opened a whole new problem.

Luca was a carter in those days, who in the course of his business visited every neighborhood in this city, and his word carried weight with Draghicchio, who believed in the things of this world and the authority of the opinions of men. Still, when all was said and done Luca was himself just a man, and his word settled nothing for Georgio, and so on the corner or on the porch of the church and through every mood and every emotion wherever men might meet, the talk went on.

Now, some said it was not talk so much as argument and they weren't friends so much as enemies, for Draghicchio was of an old family, and his people traced their descent from the ancient kings, and his talk took on a certain air, as if to say that his family had always preferred salmon roe to anchovies, a matter of taste, and that was enough for him. Georgio lay emphasis on the practical side of a matter, as on how much a thing weighed or cost rather than on matters of taste and tradition, but Draghicchio passed all this by and closed his ears to it as to a simpleminded thing, which served only to make Georgio speak louder and at greater length.

Georgio, for that matter, claimed that his people were just as old as his neighbor's, as which of us is not of Adam's kind, "a long history, but nothing to boast about," and when Draghicchio spoke of the past and of what his people had always done, Georgio made gestures to express impatience with this, as if he meant to erase all these words and all the past together and bring the thing back to the point, which was tomorrow.

"Give me tomorrow!" he would say in the face of the difficulties Draghicchio posed.

For to Draghicchio the things of this earth were more complex than our hopes or our dollars and cents, and indeed when he spoke he tended to bounce on his toes till he gave the appearance of trying to express all sides of the matter, while Georgio planted his feet like the roots of a tree and did not budge, on into the night and all the next day, too, if need be—yes, by heaven, because the principle was the thing! Saying this, he stamped his foot on the cobbles like Luca's horse. Perhaps about this one thing they agreed, for Draghicchio believed in principle, too, even though it was a different principle, and there things stood.

Now, to argue about the anchovies or the ripeness of plums and where the value lay, whether on the green side of ripe or on the brown, that was one thing. For Georgio held stock in the green side because his hope lay all in tomorrow, and that was why he counted pennies and weighed his flour, but Draghicchio believed in the past and in the brown side of ripe, and so a little more or less in weight or silver coin, what was that to what had already transpired in this the fallen world, and if a man couldn't see that, there was no sense in speaking with him! For always when they spoke of plums or pennyweight, philosophy was close behind.

"It's not where a thing has been that we're talking about," Georgio would be heard to insist. "It's where it goes. For a brick is not a brick unless it fits into a building. Otherwise it's just in the way."

"In the way of what, may I ask?" said his friend, spitting his words to make his point.

"That's what we're talking about!" cried Georgio. "The building that brick can build. That's why the plum must be a little green, because before I eat, I go home, wash hands, put on napkin, sit down to bless the meat—"

"You save that plum, but for what?" said Draghicchio. "This you cannot say."

"For tomorrow!" Georgio cried, who had reached the limit.

Draghicchio shook his head and frowned, and when he opened his mouth it was not to loose more words but to eat a plum to demonstrate that the time for such things was now, not tomorrow, because who knows what tomorrow might bring! Tomorrow! He crossed himself at the thought of it and launched into a catalogue of things that happen—floods, tempests, fires, tornadoes—and he rose up on his toes as he spoke as if he would look over the tops of the houses to see these things approach, or perhaps depart which had already done their dirty work.

Seventeen plums they ate to settle this point of philosophy there before de Palma's market, and when de Palma sent his wife out with the bill, they looked at her as if she were crazy and did not heed her cries of "Communist!" at their back, and their wives had to come into the street to rescue them, Mrs. Draghicchio swearing that if her husband had eaten his weight in plums it was only because de Palma had cheated him time out of mind, and Mrs. Georgio that her husband never ate plums anyway, never liked them, because they were too dear by the half dozen. In the street wives are a practical race and will say anything in a moment of need, but back in the house, inside the door, it is another story. Draghicchio passed it by with his hand, and Georgio went away holding his heart, as if all those plums going down the hatch had given him the heartburn, and the point of philosophy remained unsettled.

Sometimes their arguments seemed to go together like vinegar and oil in a salad, and sometimes they grated like sand, for always they were on the opposite side, and never was this so clear as when they discussed the character of daughters. For from wives come children, and sometimes, heaven help us, those children are daughters.

It so happened that Georgio and Draghicchio had girl-children born to them at the same time, and when each heard the news, each rejoiced that his friend was in the same boat. For everyone knows that bringing daughters into this world is a perilous matter, and one slip, and your soul is lost. For if your daughter smiles, she is in danger of becoming a loose woman and losing her hope for the future, and if she frowns, then sure as nothing she will find no husband for her bed and be a burden to her parents and drive them to the grave.

Georgio's child was a merry wench who chortled at the slightest thing, which spoke to Georgio of the devil's own license. To Draghicchio, on the other hand, it spoke of a melancholy love of this world, as if perchance the place were not so bad and had fallen not so far as he might have supposed. His own daughter, much to his regret, was fretful in her disposition with crying for her mother's teat, and when Draghicchio looked at her little face all wrinkled up and swollen with tears, it made his steps heavy down the hall, while Georgio loved this child's grave demeanor till it made his soul light. And they would have traded baskets then and there, if it had not been that their wives, fond creatures, loved each the fruit of her womb with all her heart.

So when Draghicchio heard his neighbor bemoan his daughter's laughter, calling her "sinful woman" and "low female type," it stung his heart; and when Georgio saw his neighbor pull a long face and look like a lemon, all wizened up like fallen fruit before his grave girl, it made his thoughts boil.

"A man like you," Georgio cried, "you don't deserve to father this saint. Fatherhood is for those who believe in something."

"The lord save me, but am I not Sicilian!" said Draghicchio. "Don't I know what saints do and tomorrow brings!"

That is the way they spoke, with passion, because each believed in what he said.

"It may be that you were Sicilian once," Georgio said, "but this is America, the land of tomorrow, and that other is past and gone which you were. Why did you come here if that other was so wonderful! You came as I did, because there you starve and here you have hope. Now you are American like me!"

He thumped his chest at this point of pride, and once again their wives had to show their faces on the street, urging and cajoling them to break off this loose talk and return home, Mrs. Draghicchio with promises of wine and dried fruit and cheese to eat, Mrs. Georgio with "something beneficial" on the radio.

"But let me ask you one thing," Draghicchio said over his shoulder. "What is it you hope for tomorrow? What, in your mind, will come?"

Georgio thought, but no words could express his wish, and the more he thought the longer his face grew. There were so many things, and they were so hard to say.

"Is it Goodness?" said Draghicchio softly, seeing the difficulty his friend was in. "Is it Beauty and Truth?" leading the conversation in a sly way.

Georgio nodded, for he found in these words a lovely thought.

"But don't you see, my friend, the lie of it?" said Draghicchio, laughing in the sureness of his triumph. "Do things in time grow more lovely or less? Do they grow better or worse? Why, look at yourself, my friend. Look at me. Are we better men than we were? Are we more beautiful? No, there is no good to come for it. Don't we know from the past that hope is a lie?"

For the thing Draghicchio hated most in life was to pretend that he was not pretending and to hope for what he knew could not be, which tasted to his palate not like the rotten fruit he bought at de Palma's market, which everything was, but like these things you buy in a store which you don't know quite how to describe, but they are nothing. Now, a lie is one thing, and there is great virtue in it, but to pretend to ourselves that we do not lie when we know we do. . . .

Perhaps his old friend had eaten that which did not sit well in his belly, but as Georgio harkened to his neighbor's words, a vacancy opened up in his look, and in that moment he saw far far into the future, as far as there is to see, and when he opened his mouth to speak, no words came out, and he staggered in a little circle as if his legs had all gone stiff or he meant to prove the world round. Perhaps he saw that his hope was truly not of this world, for he put his hand to his heart to express the heaviness of his thought, and dropped down on the sidewalk dead.

That happened before they tore down the church and we all got rich.

Draghicchio had won, but as a man who loved the truth, he came to hate its triumph even more than he had hated a lie. He found that without his friend he had nothing more in this world to say, and he faded into the background of our neighborhood, and I would see him sunning himself on a park bench or on a chair inside the door at Bella's fish market, but never did I hear him utter another word. Then I ceased even to see him, no more than you see a crack in a wall that you pass every day for a hundred years, and he became solid and predictable like the stones under your feet to which you pay no attention except when the earth quakes.

I remember nothing more about him until years later in the new neighborhood, late one afternoon, I heard children calling outside the door: "Mr. Georgio, Mr. Georgio." It roused me from the dream of what I was doing, and from the door I saw old Draghicchio and his wife pass down the street arm in arm very slowly, for he was truly old now, and he handed out of his pocket candied chickpeas to the children, who cried in a chorus: "Thank you, Mr. Georgio. Mr. Georgio, thank you."

I rubbed my eyes, because I did not know if I had forgotten who lived and who died. But, no, this was Draghicchio whom they called by his old friend's name. His wife, you see, always wore great hats, and the one she had on her head, piled with flowers like a cornucopia, brought it all back. Somehow to these children he had become his old adversary.

He tipped his hat and smiled shyly as he passed my door, and the look on his face was of apology, as if he wished me to forgive him for this one small lie.

I bowed to him and her, and they went slowly on their way. But it occurred to me that if the grave Georgio should be remembered by a generation of children as a kind old man passing out candied chickpeas, then perhaps there is more mercy in this world than we like to think. You couldn't call it justice. It was the mercy of Draghicchio for his old friend, the American.

His daughter has "gone to the church," as they say of those who take Christ for their husband, while the daughter of Georgio long since married a sailor and moved away. And Luca the carter? He got rich, too, and became a big man in trucking, a regular American.

Afterword

"POETRY makes nothing happen," W.H. Auden once remarked and the same, I suppose, might be said of stories, though his dictum is true of both only to the extent that we define happenings as external events occurring "out there," in the busy world of trouble and transaction. For in the other world, the one "in there," in the mind, stories do indeed make things happen, causing instantaneous but irrevocable shifts in our perceptions, in the ways we think and feel about the world. Such changes are one of the effects of Michael Mooney's fiction. We cannot read "Laughter" without thinking, at the end, differently about the essence of comedy. We cannot read "The Strange Heart" without shifting our notions about how the young first discover and explore their sexuality. We do not, however, come to these changes by way of a bulky, philosophical effort. It is true of the best fiction that it moves us from one place to another without making us much aware of the passage, and that at the end of the journey the light is just perceptibly different, tinted perhaps with a shade of mystery and magic.

We come to such a locale in Mooney's fictional world by being ushered through a realm that is almost medieval in nature, one that seems at first very remote from our contemporary experience. Just what are the characteristics of this medieval world set unexpectedly against a background of factory warehouses, corner grocery stores, and steamy kitchens? First, there is the fickleness of fate, the swift and arbitrary way in which our fortunes can falter. It is expressed in "Thief" as "the ease with which a man's luck can change, and fate and the world go against him," in "Laughter" as "a world governed by unmitigable agents," and in "The Popcorn Stand" in the person of the lady from the Bureau of Relocation, a modern version of one of the three fates, complete with scroll, fixing on paper the length of the old way of life.

Second, there is the emphasis upon the taint and corruption of this life in contradistinction to the lofty ideals, the life of principles lived out in the seclusion of the mind. In "Laughter" the comedian tries desperately to get his audience to share his more elevated vision. For the Serbs in "The Popcorn Stand," "You were sired in contempt, an afternoon or a morning's fling in the long life of your father's disappointment." Joey, in "Thief" casts aside this flawed world to dedicate himself to the visionary ideal and it is the cause of his undoing, for in Mooney's stories, as in Blake, imagination untempered by experience is destined to fail; it is a kind of innocence. Joey loses both riches and the woman of his heart because he is duped by the sophist rhetoric of his father or, more accurately, by his father's realism, for in the end his father's ways are those of the world and Joey must go forth to confront them. In "Women" the man of high ideals is Zak, despite the trappings of business that surround him. Zak spars with the world of social corruption—"Where the judge becomes a justice by the size of his contribution to the mayor's campaign."—as well as with the unending brigade of lesser men, those minor beings seeking relief from worry or debt of their own making—in short, men lacking principle and Zak's heroic mold. He is a superior man by virtue of his guile and by virtue of his vision of the world as a waiting scheme only needing a gifted man to crack it.

Third, there is the division of things into sharp dualities, the world of day and that of night, of ledger books and imagination, of people into pirates or dragons, gentlemen or snakes. In "Voyages" we begin to explore one of the book's most pervasive themes in such terms: the nature of men and women. In a letter written during the preparation of this volume, Mooney has this to say about his chief preoccupation:

> The stories focus on the relationship between men and women, husbands and wives, and from the point of view of the man, on how the woman gets identified with the world in general, its recalcitrance, its indifference, its otherness. This can be very troubling, very poignant, but also very funny. "Voyages" reflects one side of it; "Snow" the other.

This is true, but beyond it, Mooney moves to invert our traditional notions of men and women. In the stories, women are the creatures of imagination and heroic effort more often than men. Men stake out a practical claim on the necessities of life that women are more likely to scorn than to appreciate. In "Voyages" women are pirates, and pirates are a "more than natural phenomenon; pirates take a philosophical stance to the world." They are laughed at as impractical, they reject the niceties of civilization, they give themselves wholly to imagination. The unnamed wife of the story contains in her something deep within all women. She ignores dishes and children, she sits self-absorbed with her feet propped up on the table. But she is not lazy; she is only assuming her characteristic spiritual perspective on the world, lost in thought about the moons of Jupiter. The "otherness" Mooney mentions is certainly present in the story; woman is a species apart, living by different rules beyond the pale of male understanding.

In "Mr. Georgio" the dualities take another form—that of contrasting and uncompromising views of life. Mr. Georgio represents the American future; he is a practical and serious man, dedicated to the business of success and forever exclaiming "Give me tomorrow!" His comrade and adversary Mr. Draghicchio is, on the other hand, an old world cynic who believes hope is a lie and loves the truth, though we discover in his final act, he loves it less than mercy. That the two men are opposed is less significant than the philosophical uniqueness of each. They represent distinct ways that people approach the world, though the triumph of Draghicchio's humanity suggests that the author intends us to have a greater sympathy with his tempered pessimism. The contrasts of character here are so stark because Mooney, in isolating the qualities of the philosophical self, shows how these qualities can have serious consequences outside the world of the self, in the area of actual affairs.

Such consequences are further explored in the story "The Masculine Principle." Here, the tense conflict of theoretical ideologies, presented in the arguments between Professor Eliot and Porteous, gives rise to a series of events that shake the foundations of the family's middle class decorum. Culture and conversation are losing out to unfettered appetite and beer-drinking parties. John Porteous' return to a more primitive masculine state, vicariously through the antics of his dog, is a triumph of anarchistic freedom over social formality, over what is, by implication, the feminine principle. Such a shifting conception of the female is one of the paradoxes of Mooney's vision.

The characters that people these stories, as the previous discussion I hope makes clear, are an unusual lot. They seem to strive against "the variety and awesome power of people and circumstance and events" in a kind of private battle that is as much against a part of themselves as it is against a recalcitrant, external reality. They are continually betrayed by the eternal promissory notes of life which offer everything but actually deliver very little. These wandering souls often operate outside the accepted boundaries of behavior and it is not surprising to find them variously described as outlaws, desperadoes, or questers, not content with the commonplace niches of the rest of us.

In "Laughter," the comedian's search for truth leads him into speeches against tradition as well as into genuinely lawless acts, but his mistake is chortled back at him in the laughter of the crowd. He imagines himself chosen, with a special mission as the emissary of truth. But in his quest for special designation, he is ironically transformed into the very thing he opposes: the bringer of laughter, that great leveler of men.

Were I to conclude my commentary on these stories now, they might seem to the reader philosophically interesting, even original, highly serious. I am at pains to demonstrate that this is not their essence. For Mooney's fiction is enriched throughout with a lively—at times uproarious—humor. Without this humor, the stories would not be what they are; wry and ribald accounts of our foibles as well as our aspirations, the kind of tales that recall Chaucer in their paradoxical acceptance and attack on our flawed personalities and institutions. This humor is conveyed in dialog and setting and event and is at its most compelling in "Footings for the Humanities." The story derives its humor from several sources, not the least of which is the contrast between a lofty discipline—physics—and the wholly earthly uses to which it is put by Joe Boulebays. The fine touch of the ending, in which Joe takes a swing at the humanities building which is not there, is a good illustration of the whimsical extremes which Mooney is capable of creating.

All this is achieved in a structure which is at once distant and immediate. The occasionally elevated and poetic dialog, the appeal to oracle (Gena in "Squid Soup"), the archetypal character of Mr. Georgio or the lady of the Bureau of Relocation—all this reminds us of the world of the folktale, with the focus and concentration on timeless truths and universal types, rather than modern fiction with its careful character delineation and existential despair. And if we grasp folktale in its most original sense, we will see even more clearly the similarities it shares with Mooney's fiction: both are stories which identify and explore the survival of archaic beliefs and customs in a modern age; and in both the purpose is to reconstruct the spiritual history of the race through the study of the ways of the common people.

But the stories are not relics. I said at the beginning that Mooney's stories were seemingly remote from the world of today, but after we have finished reading them, I do not believe that we can maintain that this is so. The characters live and love and work in ways we recognize. They are stuck in an historical frame identical to our own and they act in ways which we are willing to attribute, if not to ourselves, then at least to our neighbors. Though there seem in the stories supernatural or magical events, when we are pressed to recall them, we find they are more of our world than we can quite explain. And this is, perhaps, wherein we may fix this collection's charm.

Richard Meade
Chicago, 1980

About the Author

Michael Mooney received his doctorate from Edinburgh University in Medieval and Renaissance literature. He lives in Milwaukee with his wife, Kathy, and their daughter, Sheila, where he works for a real estate management firm. His first book, a novella called "Names," appeared last fall, published by Treacle Press.

About the Illustrator

Peter Balestrieri studied in Florence with the painter Pietro Annigoni. He lives in Milwaukee with his wife, Nancy, and their children, Joe and Andrea, where he and Mooney are neighbors. Although he has had numerous shows and exhibitions, this is his first group of illustrations for a book.

Story
Press

P. O. Box 10040
Chicago, Ill. 60610

Story Press is a small, non-profit publishing company committed primarily to the short story. We publish the Illinois Writers Series, called "a series to watch" by *Publishers Weekly,* as well as books by authors outside of our home state. Our hope is to bring recognition to writers working in a genre increasingly neglected by the commercial houses. Our previous books have won literary awards and we think our efforts are appreciated by the reading public. This book has been produced entirely without public funding, so your support is crucial.

DATE DUE
